"Ar

Elena cupped Nick's ... smile. "I'm fine."

One long finger stroked down her cheek, sending a raw shimmer through her. "Then why do I get the feeling that you're not quite comfortable with this?"

"Probably because I haven't done *this* in a while."

Something flared in his gaze. "How long?"

"Uh—around six years, I guess."

He said something soft beneath his breath. "Six years ago you slept with me."

The breath caught in her throat. "I'm surprised you remember."

"I'm not likely to forget," he said quietly, "since you were a virgin."

For a split second she was afraid he might abandon the whole idea of making love, so she took a deep breath and boldly trailed a hand down his chest. "I'm not a virgin now."

He trapped her hand beneath his, then used it to pull her close so that she found herself half-sprawled across his chest. "Good."

* * *

Just One More Night
is part of The Pearl House series: Business and passion collide when two dynasties forge ties bound by love

* * *

If you're on Twitter,
tell us what you think of Harlequin Desire!
#harlequindesire

Dear Reader,

This was originally one of those books writers hear about when they start out writing—the book that just won't fly and needs to be put aside, preferably in a bottom drawer where it gathers dust and is forgotten.

The problem was that I really liked the premise of my bottom-drawer book, and when Elena Lyon presented herself to me as a character in *A Perfect Husband,* I saw the opportunity to dust off the story.

Elena and her fatal attraction to gorgeous bad boy Nick Messena provided the perfect basis to make my original premise, which involved a wager and a love quiz, work. With a past that had thrown up deeply emotional barriers, I finally had a *real* story. The icing on the cake was the fun that Elena brought. Tired of being on the relationship back foot, she made herself over, got herself a boyfriend and even changed careers. A modern-day Cinderella, she dared to want the very best for herself—to decide that she deserved true love.

I hope you enjoy this latest Pearl House story.

Fiona

JUST ONE
MORE NIGHT

—

FIONA BRAND

Recycling programs
for this product may
not exist in your area.

ISBN-13: 978-0-373-73298-2

JUST ONE MORE NIGHT

Copyright © 2014 by Fiona Gillibrand

HARLEQUIN®
™ www.Harlequin.com

Printed in U.S.A.

Books by Fiona Brand

Harlequin Desire

*A Breathless Bride #2154
*A Tangled Affair #2166
*A Perfect Husband #2178
*The Fiancée Charade #2238
*Just One More Night #2285

Harlequin Romantic Suspense

O'Halloran's Lady #1733

Silhouette Romantic Suspense

Cullen's Bride #914
Heart of Midnight #977
Blade's Lady #1023
Marrying McCabe #1099
Gabriel West: Still the One #1219
High-Stakes Bride #1403

Silhouette Books

Sheiks of Summer
   "Kismet"

*The Pearl House

Other titles by this author available in ebook format.

FIONA BRAND

lives in the sunny Bay of Islands, New Zealand. Now that both her sons are grown, she continues to love writing books and gardening. After a life-changing time in which she met Christ, she has undertaken study for a bachelor of theology and has become a member of The Order of St. Luke, Christ's healing ministry.

To the Lord, whose "word is a lamp unto my feet, and a light unto my path."
—*Psalms* 119

For God so loved the world that he gave his one and only Son, that whoever believes in him shall not perish but have eternal life.
—*John* 3:16

Many thanks to Stacy Boyd, Allison Carroll and all of the editorial staff who work so hard to help shape and polish each book, and always do a fabulous job.

One

Elena Lyon would never get a man in her life until she surgically removed every last reminder of Nick Messena from hers!

Number one on her purge list was getting rid of the beach villa located in Dolphin Bay, New Zealand, in which she had spent one disastrous, passionate night with Messena.

As she strolled down one of Auckland's busiest streets, eyes peeled for the real estate agency she had chosen to handle the sale, a large sign emblazoned with the name Messena Construction shimmered into view, seeming to float in the brassy summer heat.

Automatic tension hummed, even though the likelihood that Nick, who spent most of his time overseas, was at the busy construction site was small.

Although, the sudden conviction that he was there, and watching her, was strong enough to stop her in her tracks.

Taking a deep breath, she dismissed the overreaction which was completely at odds with her usual calm precision and girded herself to walk past the brash, noisy work site. Gaze averted from a trio of bare-chested construction workers, Elena decided she couldn't wait to sell the beach villa. Every time she visited, it seemed to hold whispering echoes of the intense emotions that, six years ago, had been her downfall.

Emotions that hadn't appeared to affect the dark and dangerously unreliable CEO of Messena Construction in the slightest.

The rich, heady notes of a tango emanating from her handbag distracted Elena from an embarrassingly loud series of whistles and catcalls.

A breeze whipped glossy, dark tendrils loose from her neat French pleat as she retrieved the phone. Pushing her glasses a little higher on the delicate bridge of her nose, she peered at the number glowing on her screen.

Nick Messena.

Her heart slammed once, hard. The sticky heat and background hum of Friday afternoon traffic dissolved and she was abruptly transported back six years....

To the dim heat of what had then been her aunt Katherine's beach villa, tropical rain pounding on the roof. Nick Messena's muscular, tanned body sprawled heavily across hers—

Cheeks suddenly overwarm, she checked the phone, which had stopped ringing. A message flashed on the screen. She had voice mail.

Her jaw locked. It had to be a coincidence that Nick had rung this afternoon when she was planning one of her infrequent trips back to Dolphin Bay.

Her fingers tightened on the utilitarian black cell, the perfect no-nonsense match for her handbag. Out of the blue, Nick had started ringing her a week ago at her apartment in Sydney. Unfortunately, she had been off guard enough to actually pick up the first call, then mesmerized enough by the sexy timbre of his voice that she'd been incapable of slamming the phone down.

To make matters worse, somehow, she had ended up agreeing to meet him for dinner, as if the searing hours she'd spent locked in his arms all those years ago had never happened.

Of course, she hadn't gone, and she hadn't canceled, either. She had stood him up.

Behaving in such a way, without manners or consideration, had gone against the grain. But the jab of guilt had been swamped by a warming satisfaction that finally, six years on, Messena had gotten a tiny taste of the disappointment she had felt.

The screen continued to flash its message.

Don't listen. Just delete the message.

The internal directives came a split second too late. Her thumb had already stabbed the button that activated her voice mail.

Nick's deep, curt voice filled her ear, shooting a hot tingle down her spine and making her stomach clench.

This message was simple, his number and the same arrogant demand he'd left on her answerphone a number of times since their initial conversation: *Call me.*

For a split second the busy street and the brassy glare of the sun glittering off cars dissolved in a red mist.

After six years? During which time he had utterly ignored her existence and the fact that he had ditched her after just one night.

Like that was going to happen.

Annoyed with herself for being weak enough to listen to the message, she dropped the phone back into her purse and stepped off the curb. No matter how much she had once wanted Nick to call, she had never fallen into the trap of chasing after a man she knew was not interested in her personally.

To her certain knowledge Nick Messena had only ever wanted two things from her. Lately, it was the recovery of a missing ring that Nick had mistakenly decided his father had gifted to her aunt. A scenario that resurrected the scandalous lie that her aunt Katherine—the Messena family's housekeeper—had been engaged in a steamy affair with Stefano Messena, Nick's father.

Six years ago, Nick's needs had been a whole lot simpler: he had wanted sex.

The blast of a car horn jerked her attention back to the busy street. Adrenaline rocketing through her veins, Elena hurried out of the path of a bus and stepped into the air-conditioned coolness of an exclusive mall.

She couldn't believe how stupid she had been to walk across a busy street without taking careful note of the traffic. Almost as stupid as she'd been six years ago on her birthday when she'd been lonely enough to break every personal rule she'd had and agree to a blind date.

The date, organized by so-called friends, had turned out to be with Messena, the man she'd had a hopeless crush on for most of her teenage years.

At age twenty-two, with a double degree in business and psychology, she should have been wary of such an improbable situation. Messena had been hot and in demand. With her long dark hair and creamy skin, and her legs—her best feature—she had been passable. But with her propensity to be just a little plump, she hadn't been in Messena's league.

Despite knowing that, her normal common sense had let her down. She had made the fatal mistake of believing in the heated gleam in Nick's gaze and the off-the-register passion. She had thought that Messena, once branded a master of seduction by one notorious tabloid, was sincere.

Heart still pumping too fast, she strolled through the rich, soothing interior of the mall, which, as luck would have it, was the one that contained the premises for Coastal Realty.

The receptionist—a lean, elegant redhead—showed her into Evan Cutler's office.

Cutler, who specialized in waterfront developments and central city apartments, shot to his feet as she stepped through the door. Shadow and light flickered over an expanse of dove-gray carpet, alerting Elena to the fact that Cutler wasn't the sole occupant of the room.

A second man, large enough to block the sunlight that would otherwise have flooded through a window, turned, his black jacket stretched taut across broad shoulders, his tousled dark hair shot through with lighter streaks that gleamed like hot gold.

A second shot of adrenaline zinged through her veins. *"You."*

Nick Messena. Six feet two inches of sleekly muscled male, with a firm jaw and the kind of clean, chiseled cheekbones that still made her mouth water.

He wasn't male-model perfect. Despite the fact that he was a wealthy businessman, somewhere along the way he had gotten a broken nose and a couple of nicks on one cheekbone. The battered, faintly dangerous look, combined with a dark five-o'clock shadow—and that wicked body—and there was no doubting he was potent. A dry, low-key charm and a reputation with women that scorched, and Nick was officially hot.

Her stomach sank when she noticed the phone in his hand.

Eyes a light, piercing shade of green, clashed with hers. "And you didn't pick up my call, because…?"

The low, faintly gravelly rasp of his voice, as if he had just rolled out of a tangled, rumpled bed, made her stomach tighten. "I was busy."

"I noticed. You should check the street before you cross."

Fiery irritation canceled out her embarrassment and other more disturbing sensations that had coiled in the pit of her stomach. Positioned at the window, Nick would have had a clear view of her walking down the street as he had phoned. "Since when have you been so concerned about my welfare?"

He slipped the phone into his jacket pocket. "Why wouldn't I be? I've known you and your family most of my life."

The easy comment, as if their families were on friendly terms and there hadn't been a scandal, as if he hadn't slept with her, made her bristle. "I guess if anything happened to me, you might not get what you want."

The second the words were out Elena felt ashamed. As ruffled and annoyed as she was by Nick, she didn't for a moment think he was that cold and calculating. If the assertion that her aunt and Stefano Messena had been having an affair when they were killed in a car accident, *the same night she and Nick had made love,* had hurt the Lyon family, it went without saying it had hurt the Messenas.

Her jaw tightened at Nick's lightning perusal of her olive-green dress and black cotton jacket, and the way his attention lingered on her one and only vice, her shoes. The clothes were designer labels and expensive, but she was suddenly intensely aware that the dark colors in the middle of summer looked dull and boring. Unlike the shoes, which were strappy and outrageously feminine, the crisp tailoring and straight lines were more about hiding curves than displaying them.

Nick's gaze rested briefly on her mouth. "And what is it, exactly, that you think I want?"

A question that shouldn't be loaded, but suddenly was, made her breath hitch in her throat. Although the thought that Nick could possibly have any personal interest in her now was ridiculous.

And she was absolutely not interested in him. Despite the hot looks, *GQ* style and killer charm, he had a blunt, masculine toughness that had always set her subtly on edge.

Although she could never allow herself to forget that, through some weird alchemy, that same quality had once cut through her defenses like a hot knife through butter. "I already told you I have no idea where your lost jewelry is."

"But you are on your way back to Dolphin Bay."

"I have better reasons for going there than looking for your mythical lost ring." She lifted her chin, abruptly certain that Nick's search for the ring, something that the female members of his family could have done, was a ploy and that he had another, shadowy, agenda. Although what that agenda could be, she had no clue. "More to the point, how did you find out I would be here?"

"You haven't been returning my calls, so I rang Zane."

Her annoyance level increased another notch that Nick had intruded even further into her life by calling his cousin, and her boss, Zane Atraeus. "Zane is in Florida."

Nick's expression didn't alter. "Like I said, you haven't returned my calls, and you didn't turn up for our...appointment in Sydney. You left me no choice."

Elena's cheeks warmed at his blunt reference to the

fact that she had failed to meet him for what had sounded more like a date than a business meeting at one of Sydney's most expensive restaurants.

She had never in her life missed an appointment, or even been late for one, but the idea that Nick's father had paid her aunt off with jewelry, *the standard currency for a mistress,* had been deeply insulting. "I told you over the phone, I don't believe your father gave Aunt Katherine anything. Why would he?"

His expression was oddly neutral. "They were having an affair."

She made an effort to control the automatic fury that gripped her at Nick's stubborn belief that her aunt had conducted a sneaky, underhanded affair with her employer.

Quite apart from the fact that her aunt had considered Nick's mother, Luisa Messena, to be her friend, she had been a woman of strong morals. And there was one powerful, abiding reason her aunt would never have gotten involved with Stefano, or any man.

Thirty years ago Katherine Lyon had fallen in love, completely, irrevocably, and he had *died.*

In the Lyon family the legend of Katherine's unrequited love was well respected. Lyons were not known for being either passionate or tempestuous. They were more the steady-as-you-go type of people who tended to choose solid careers and marry sensibly. In days gone by they had been admirable servants and thrifty farmers. Unrequited love, or love lost in any form was a novelty.

Elena didn't know who Aunt Katherine's lover had been because her aunt had point-blank refused to talk about him. All she knew was that her aunt, an exceptionally beautiful woman, had remained determinedly single and had stated she would never love again.

Elena's fingers tightened on the strap of her handbag. "No. They were not having an affair. Lyon women are not, and never have been, the playthings of wealthy men."

Cutler cleared his throat. "I see you two have met."

Elena turned her gaze on the real estate agent, who was a small, balding man with a precise manner. There were no confusing shades with Cutler, which was why she had chosen him. He was factual and efficient, attributes she could relate to in her own career as a personal assistant.

Although, it seemed the instant she had any contact with Nick Messena, her usual calm, methodical process evaporated and she found herself plunged into the kind of passionate emotional excess that was distinctly un-Lyon-like. "We're acquainted."

Nick's brows jerked together. "I seem to remember it was a little more than that."

Elena gave up the attempt to avoid the confrontation Nick was angling for and glared back. "If you were a gentleman, you wouldn't mention the past."

"As I recall from a previous conversation, I'm no gentleman."

Elena blushed at his reference to the accusation she had flung at him during a chance meeting in Dolphin Bay, a couple of months after their one night together. That he was arrogant and ruthless and emotionally incapable of sustaining a relationship. "I don't see why I should help drag the Lyon name through the mud one more time just because you want to get your hands on some clunky old piece of jewelry you've managed to lose."

His brows jerked together. "I didn't lose anything, and you already know that the missing piece of jewelry is a diamond ring."

And knowing the Messena family and their extreme wealth, the diamond would be large, breathtakingly expensive and probably old. "Aunt Katherine would have zero interest in a diamond ring. In case you didn't notice, she was something of a feminist and she almost never wore jewelry. Besides, if she was having a *secret* affair with your father, what possible interest would she have in wearing an expensive ring that proclaimed that fact?"

Nick's gaze cooled perceptibly. "Granted. Nevertheless, the ring is gone."

Cutler cleared his throat and gestured that she take a seat. "Mr. Messena has expressed interest in the villa you've inherited in Dolphin Bay. He proposed a swap with one of his new waterfront apartments here in Auckland, which is why I invited him to this meeting."

Elena suppressed her knee-jerk desire to say that, as keen as she was to sell, there was no way she would part with the villa to a Messena. "That's very interesting," she said smoothly. "But at the moment I'm keeping my options open."

Still terminally on edge at Nick's brooding presence, Elena debated stalking out of the office in protest at the way her meeting with Cutler had been hijacked.

In the end, feeling a little sorry for Cutler, she sat in one of the comfortable leather seats he had indicated. She soothed herself with the thought that if Nick Messena, the quintessential entrepreneur and businessman, wanted to make her an offer, then she should hear it, even if only for the pleasure of saying no.

Instead of sitting in the other available chair, Nick propped himself on the edge of Cutler's desk. The casual lounging position had the effect of making him look even larger and more muscular as he loomed over her.

"It's a good deal. The apartments are in the Viaduct and they're selling fast."

The Viaduct was the waterfront area just off the central heart of the city, which overlooked the marina. It was both picturesque and filled with wonderful restaurants and cafés. As an area, it was at the top of her wish list because it would be so easy to rent out the apartment. A trade would eliminate the need to take out a mortgage to afford a waterfront apartment, something the money from selling the villa wouldn't cover completely.

Nick's gaze skimmed her hair, making her aware that, during her dash across the road, silky wisps had escaped to trail and cling to her cheeks and neck. "I'll consider a straight swap."

Elena stiffened and wondered if Nick was reading her mind. A swap would mean she wouldn't have to go into debt, which was tempting. "The villa has four bedrooms. I'd want at least two in an apartment."

He shrugged. "I'll throw in a third bedroom, a dedicated parking space, and access to the pool and fitness center."

Three bedrooms. Elena blinked as a rosy future without the encumbrance of a mortgage opened up. She caught the calculating gleam in Nick's eye and realized the deal was too good. There could be only one reason for that. It had strings.

He was deliberately dangling the property because he wanted her to help him find the missing ring, which he no doubt thought, since she didn't personally have it, must still be in the old villa somewhere.

Over her dead body.

Elena swallowed the desire to grasp at what was an exceptionally good real estate deal.

She couldn't do it if it involved selling out in any way

to a Messena. Maybe it was a subtle point, but after the damage done to her aunt's reputation, even if it was years in the past, *and after her own seduction,* she was determined to make a stand.

Lyon property was not for sale to a Messena, just like Lyon women were not for sale. She met Nick's gaze squarely. "No."

Cutler's disbelief was not mirrored on Nick's face. His gaze was riveted on her, as if in that moment he found her completely, utterly fascinating.

Another small heated tingle shot down her spine and lodged in her stomach.

As if, in some perverse way, he had liked it that she had said no.

Two

Elena dragged her gaze from the magnetic power of Nick's and fought the crazy urge to stay and continue sparring with him.

Pushing to her feet, she bid Cutler good day, picked up her handbag and stepped out the door. Nick was close enough behind her that the sudden overpowering sense that she was being pursued sent another hot, forbidden thrill zinging through her.

The door snapped closed. Nick's firm tread confirmed that he was in pursuit and the faint, heady whiff of his cologne made her stomach clench. Clamping down on the wimpy feeling that she was prey and Nick was a large, disgruntled predator, Elena lengthened her stride and walked briskly past the receptionist out into the mall.

She had just stepped out of air-conditioned coolness into the humid heat of the street when a large tanned hand curled briefly around her upper arm. "What I don't get is why you're still so angry."

Elena spun and faced Nick, although that was a mistake because she was suddenly close enough that she could see a pulse jumping along the line of his jaw.

She tilted her chin to meet his gaze, unbearably aware that while she was quite tall at five foot eight, Nick was several inches taller and broad enough that he actually made her feel feminine and fragile. "You shouldn't have crashed my meeting with Cutler or tried to pressure me when you knew ahead of time how I felt."

There was an odd, vibrating pause. "I'm sorry if I hurt you six years ago, but after what happened that night it couldn't be any other way."

His words, the fact that he obviously thought she had fallen for him six years ago, dropped into a pool of silence that seemed to expand and spread around them, blotting out the street noise. She dragged her gaze from the taut planes of his cheekbones, the inky crescents of his lashes. "Are you referring to the accident, or the fact that you were already involved with someone else called *Tiffany?*" A girlfriend he'd apparently had stashed away in Dubai.

Nick frowned. "The relationship with Tiffany was already ending."

Elena found herself staring at the V of bronzed flesh bared by the pale peach T-shirt Nick was wearing beneath his black jacket. Peach. It was a feminine color, but on Nick the color looked sexy and hot, emphasizing the tough, stubbled line of his jaw and the cool gleam of his eyes. "I read about Tiffany in an article that was published a whole month later."

She would never forget because the statement that Nick Messena and his gorgeous model girlfriend were in love had finally convinced her that a relationship with him had never been viable.

"You shouldn't believe anything printed in a tabloid. We broke up as soon as I got back to Dubai."

Elena ruthlessly suppressed the sudden, wild, improbable notion that Nick had ended his relationship with Tiffany because of her.

That was the kind of flawed thinking that had seen her climbing into bed with him in the first place. "That still didn't make it all right to sleep with me when you had no intention of ever following up."

A hint of color rimmed Nick's cheekbones. "No, it didn't. If you'll recall, I did apologize."

Her jaw tightened. As if it had all been a gigantic mistake. "So why, exactly, did you finish with Tiffany?"

She shouldn't have the slightest interest. Nick Messena meant nothing to her—absolutely nothing—but suddenly she desperately needed to know.

He dragged long, tanned fingers through his hair, his expression just a little bad-tempered and terminally, broodingly sexy. "How would I know why?" he growled. "Men don't know that stuff. It ended, like it always does."

She blinked at his statement that his relationships always ended. For reasons she didn't want to go into, there was something profoundly depressing in that thought.

She stared at his wide mouth and the fuller bottom lip, which was decorated with a small, jagged scar. She couldn't remember the scar being there six years ago. It suggested he had since been involved in a fight.

Probably a brawl on one of his construction sites.

Against all good sense, the heady tension she had so far failed to defuse tightened another notch. Feeling, as she was, unsettled by memories of the past, distinctly vulnerable and on edge from the blast of Nick's potent sexuality, it was not a good idea to imagine Nick Messena in warrior mode.

She dragged her gaze from his mouth and the vivid memory of what it had felt like to be kissed by Nick. "Maybe you go about things in the wrong way?"

He stared at her, transfixed. "How, exactly, should I 'go about' things?"

She took a deep breath and tried to ignore the piercing power of his gaze. "Conversation is not a bad starter." That had been something that had been distinctly lacking in their night together.

"I talk."

The gravelly irritation in his voice, the way his gaze lingered on her mouth, made her suddenly intensely aware that he, too, was remembering *that* night.

She could feel her cheeks warming all over again that she had actually offered Nick advice about improving his relationships. Advice had so far failed to be her forte, despite the psychology classes she had passed.

The heat that rose off the sidewalk and floated in the air seemed to increase in intensity, opening up every pore. Perspiration trickled down the groove of her spine and between her breasts. She longed to shrug out of the overlarge jacket, but she would rather die of heatstroke than take off one item of clothing in Nick's presence. "Women need more than sex. They need to be appreciated and...liked."

They needed to be loved.

He glanced down the street as if he was looking for someone. "I like women."

A muscular black four-wheel-drive vehicle braked to a halt in a restricted parking zone a few steps away; a horn blared. Nick lifted a hand at the driver. "That's my Jeep. If you want, I can give you a ride."

The words, the unconscious innuendo, sent another small, sensual dart through her. Climb into a vehicle with tinted windows with Nick Messena? *Never again.* "I don't need a ride."

His mouth quirked. "Just like you don't need my apartment or, I'm guessing, anything else I've got to offer."

Reaching out a finger, he gently relocated her glasses, which had once again slipped, back onto the bridge of her nose. "Why do you wear these things?"

She blinked at the small, intimate gesture. "You know I'm shortsighted."

"You should get contacts."

"Why?" But the moment she asked the question she realized what had prompted the suggestion. Fiery outrage poured through her. "So I can get a man?"

He frowned. "That wasn't what I meant, but last I heard there's nothing wrong with that…yet."

Her chin jerked up another notch. "I'm curious, what else should I change? My clothes? My shoes? How about my hair?"

"Don't change the shoes," he said on a soft growl. "Your hair is fine. It's gorgeous." He touched a loose strand with one finger. "I just don't like whatever it is you do with it."

Elena tried not to respond to the ripple of sensation that flowed out from that small touch, or to love it that he thought her hair was gorgeous. It would take more than a bit of judicious flattery to change the fact that she was hurt—and now more than a little bit mad. "It's called a French pleat." She drew a swift breath. "What else is wrong?"

He muttered something short and indistinct that she didn't quite catch. "There's no point asking me this stuff. I'm not exactly an expert."

"Meaning that I need expert help."

He pinched the bridge of his nose. "How did we get onto this? It's starting to remind me of a conversation with my sisters. And before you say it, no, I can categorically say I have never thought of you as a sister."

His gaze, as it once again dropped to her mouth, carried the same fascinated gleam she had noticed in Cutler's office. Her breath stopped in her throat at the heart-pounding thought that he was actually considering kissing her. *Despite all of her deficiencies.*

A horn blast from a delivery vehicle that wanted the restricted parking place jerked her attention away from the tough line of Nick's jaw.

A split second later the passenger door of the Jeep popped open. Nick ignored the waiting vehicle. "Damn, I did hurt you," he said softly.

Elena tried to suppress a small stab of panic that, after six years of stoically burying the past, she had clearly lost control to the point that she had revealed her vulnerability to Nick.

Pinning a bright smile on her face, she attempted to smooth out the moment by checking her watch, as if she was in a hurry. "It was a blind date. Everyone knows they never turn out."

"It wasn't a blind date for me."

The flat tone of Nick's voice jerked her gaze back to his.

Nick's expression was oddly taut. "Six years ago I happened to overhear that a friend of yours had organized a blind date for you with Geoffrey Smale. I told Smale to get lost and took his place. I knew you were the girl I was taking out, and I slept with you for one reason—because I liked you."

* * *

Broodingly, Nick climbed into the passenger-side seat of the Jeep. He shot an apologetic glance at his younger brother, Kyle, as he fastened his seat belt.

Kyle, who had a military background and a wholly unexpected genius for financial investment, accelerated away from the curb. "She looked familiar. New girl?"

"No." *Yes.*

Nick frowned at the surge of desire that that thought initiated. The kind of edgy tension he hadn't felt in a very long time—six long years to be exact. "That's Elena Lyon, from Dolphin Bay. She works for the Atraeus Group."

Kyle's expression cleared as he stopped for a set of lights. "Elena. That explains it. Zane's PA. And Katherine's niece." He sent Nick an assessing look. "Didn't think she would be your type."

Nick found himself frowning at the blunt message. Kyle knew he was the one who had found their father's car, which had slid off the road in bad weather, then rolled.

His stomach tightened on a raft of memories. Memories that had faded with time, but that were still edged with grief and guilt.

If he hadn't been in bed with Elena, captivated by the same irresistible obsession that had been at the heart of his father's supposed betrayal, *with another Lyon woman,* he might have reached the crash site in time to make a difference.

The coroner's report had claimed that both his father and Katherine had survived the impact for a time. If he had left Elena at her door that night and driven home, there was a slim possibility he might have saved them.

Nick stared broodingly at the line of traffic backed up

for a set of lights. Kyle was right. He shouldn't be thinking about Elena.

The trouble was, lately, after the discovery of a diary
and the stunning possibility that his father had not been
having an affair with Katherine, he hadn't been able to
stop thinking about Elena. "So…what is my type?"

Kyle looked wary. "Uh—they're usually blonde."

With long legs and confidence to burn. The exact opposite of Elena, with her dark eyes, her vulnerability and
enticing, sultry curves.

Feeling in need of air, Nick activated the electric window. "I don't always date blondes."

"Hey, I won't judge you."

Although, for a while, it had been blondes or nothing,
because dating dark-haired girls had cut too close to the
bone. For a couple of years the memory of his night with
Elena had been too viscerally tied into his grief and the
gnawing guilt that he had failed to save his father.

Kyle sent him the kind of neutral, male look that said
he'd noted Nick's interest in Elena, but wasn't going to
probe any further. It was the kind of unspoken accep-
tance that short-circuited the need for a conversation,
and which suited Nick.

His feelings for Elena were clear-cut enough. He
wanted her back in his bed, but he wasn't prepared to
think beyond that point.

Kyle turned into the underground parking building of
the Messena building. "Any success locating the ring?"

Nick unfastened his seat belt as Kyle pulled into a
space. "I've been asked that question a lot lately."

By his mother, his older brother, Gabriel and a selection of great-aunts and -uncles who were concerned
about the loss of an important heirloom piece. Last but

not least, the insurance assessor who, while engaged in a revaluing exercise, had discovered the ring was missing.

Climbing out of the Jeep, Nick slammed the door. "I'm beginning to feel like Frodo Baggins."

Kyle extracted his briefcase, locked the vehicle and tossed him the keys. "If that's the little guy off *Lord of the Rings,* he had prettier eyes."

"He also had friends who helped him."

Kyle grinned good-naturedly. "Cool. Just don't expect me to be one of them. My detective skills are zero. "

Nick tapped in the security PIN to access the elevator. "Anyone ever tell you you're irritating?"

"My last blonde girlfriend."

Nick hit the floor number that would take them to Gabriel's suite of offices and a discussion about diversifying his business interests. "I don't recall your last girlfriend."

Of all the Messena clan, Kyle was the quietest and the hardest to read. Maybe because of his time in Special Forces, or the fact that he had lost his wife and child to the horror of a terror attack, he had grown to be perceptibly different to them all.

"That was because I was on an overseas posting."

"She was foreign?"

"No. A military brat."

"What happened?"

He shrugged, his expression cagey. "We both moved on."

Nick studied Kyle's clean profile. With his obdurate jaw and the short, crisp cut of his hair, even in a sleek business suit he still managed to look dangerous. "So it wasn't serious."

"No."

Kyle's clear-cut indifference about his last casual relationship struck an odd chord with Nick. Kyle had cared about his wife and child, to the point that he hadn't cared about anyone since.

Nick hadn't lost a wife and child, not even close, but it was also true that for years, ever since their father had died, *and the night with Elena,* he had not been able to form a relationship.

The elevator doors slid open. Moving on automatic pilot, Nick strolled with Kyle through the familiar, hushed and expensive interior of the bank.

Normally, his social life was neatly compartmentalized and didn't impinge on the long hours he worked. But lately his social life had ground to a halt.

Dispassionately he examined the intensity of his focus on Elena, which, according to his PA, had made him irritable and terminally bad-tempered. He had considered dating, but every time he picked up the phone he found himself replacing it without making the call.

The blunt fact was that finding out that the past was not set in stone had been like opening up a Pandora's box. In that moment a raft of thoughts and emotions had hit him like a kick in the chest. Among them the stubborn, visceral need to reclaim Elena.

He couldn't fathom the need, and despite every effort, he hadn't been able to reason it away. It was just there.

The thought of making love with Elena made every muscle in his body tighten. The response, in itself, was singular. Usually when he finished a relationship it was over, his approach to dating and sex as cut-and-dried as his approach to contracting and completing a business deal.

But for some reason those few hours with Elena had stuck in his mind. Maybe the explanation was simply that what they'd shared had been over almost before it had begun. There hadn't been a cooling-off period when the usual frustrations over his commitment to his business kicked in.

But as much as he wanted Elena, bed would have to wait. His first priority had to be to obtain answers and closure. Although every time he got close to Elena the concept of closure crashed and burned.

Despite the buttoned-down clothing and schoolmarm hair, there had always been something irresistibly, tantalizingly sensual about Elena. She had probably noticed he'd been having trouble keeping his hands off her.

It was no wonder she had practically run from him in Cutler's office.

Nick had *liked* her.

A surge of delighted warmth shimmered through Elena as she strolled through a small park.

Six years ago Nick had cared enough to step in and protect her from a date that would have been uncomfortable, at best. More probably it would have ended in an embarrassing struggle, because Geoffrey Smale had a reputation for not taking no for an answer.

Feeling distinctly unsettled and on edge at this new view of the past, Elena made a beeline for the nearest park bench and sat down.

For six years she had been mad at Nick. Now she didn't know quite what to feel, except that, lurking beneath all of the confusion, being discarded by him all those years ago still hurt.

The problem was that as a teenager she'd had a thing for him. Summers spent in Dolphin Bay, visiting her aunt and watching a bronzed, muscular Nick surfing, had definitely contributed to the fascination.

Walking away from the night they'd spent together would have been easier if he had been a complete stranger, but he hadn't been. Because of her summers with her aunt at the original Lyon homestead on the beach, and because of Katherine's work for his family as a housekeeper, Elena had felt connected to Nick.

Too restless to sit, she checked her watch and strolled back in the direction of the Atraeus Hotel, where she was staying.

As she approached a set of exclusive boutiques a glass door swung open, and a sleek woman wearing a kingfisher-blue dress that showed off her perfect golden tan stepped out onto the street.

The door closed on a waft of some gorgeous perfume, and in the process Elena's reflection—that of a slightly overweight woman dressed in a plain dress and jacket, and wearing glasses—flashed back at her.

Even her handbag looked heavy and just a little boring. The only things that looked right were her shoes, which were pretty but didn't really go with the rest of her outfit.

Not just a victim, a *fashion* victim.

Nick's words came back to haunt her.

He didn't like her glasses or the way she did her hair. He hadn't mentioned her clothes, but she was seeing them through his eyes, and she was ready to admit that they were just as clunky, just as boring as the glasses and her hair.

As much as she resented his opinion, he was right. Something had to change. *She* had to change.

She could no longer immerse herself in work and avoid the fact that another birthday had just flown by. She was twenty-eight. Two more years and she would be thirty.

If she wasn't careful she would be thirty and alone.

Or she could change her life so that she would be thirty and immersed in a passionate love relationship.

Feeling electrified, as if she was standing on the edge

of a precipice, about to take a perilous leap into the unknown, she studied the elegant writing on the glass frontage of the store. A tingling sense of fate taking a hand gripped her.

It wasn't a store, exactly. It was a very exclusive and expensive health and beauty spa. The kind of place she was routinely around because her employer, the Atraeus Group, numbered a few very high-quality spa facilities among its resort properties. Of course, she had never personally utilized any of those spa facilities.

But that was the old Elena.

Her jaw firmed. She had made a decision to change. By the time she was finished, she would be, if not as pretty, at least as sleek and stylish and confident as the woman in the blue dress.

The idea gained momentum. She would no longer allow herself to feel inadequate and excluded, which would mean inner as well as outward change.

She could walk in those doors now if she wanted. She had the money. After years of saving her very good salary, she had more than enough to pay for a makeover.

Feeling a little dizzy at the notion that she didn't have to stay as she was, that she had the power to change herself, she stepped up to the exquisite white-and-gold portal. Taking a deep breath, she pushed the door wide and stepped inside.

After an initial hour-long consultation with a stylist called Giorgio, during which he had casually ticked almost every box on the interview form he had used, Elena signed on for every treatment recommended.

First up was weight loss and detox, which included a week in a secluded health spa. That was followed by a comprehensive fitness program and an introduction to her new personal trainer. A series of beauty and pamper treatments, and a comprehensive hair, makeup and wardrobe makeover completed her program.

The initial week at their spa facility would cost a staggering amount, but she was desperate.

According to Giorgio she wasn't desperate; she was worth it.

Elena wasn't about to split hairs. As long as the spa could carry out its promise and transform her, she was happy to pay.

Her heart sped up at the changes she was about to make. Hope flooded her.

The next time she saw Nick Messena, things would be different. *She* would be different.

Three

One month later, Nick Messena watched, green gaze cool, as Elena Lyon walked with measured elegance down the aisle toward him, every step precisely, perfectly timed with the beat of the Wedding March.

Mellow afternoon sunlight poured through stained glass windows, illuminating the startling changes she had made, from her long, stylishly cut, midnight-dark hair to the tips of her outrageously sexy pink high heels. Her bridesmaid's dress, a sophisticated confection of pink lace and silk that he privately thought was just a little too revealing, clung to lush, gentle curves and a mouthwateringly tiny waist.

As the bride reached the altar, Elena's gaze rested briefly on Kyle who was Gabriel's groomsman, then locked with his. With grim satisfaction, he noted that she hadn't realized he had changed roles with Kyle and taken over as Gabriel's best man. If she had, he was certain she would have very quickly and efficiently organized someone else to take her place as maid of honor.

Dragging her gaze free, Elena briskly took charge of the flower girl, Gabriel and Gemma's daughter Sanchia, who had just finished tossing rose petals. Nick's brows jerked together as he took stock of some of the changes he had barely had time to register at the prewedding dinner the previous evening. For the first time he noticed a tiny, discreet sparkle to one side of Elena's delicate nose. A piercing.

Every muscle in his body tightened at the small, exotic touch. His elusive ex-lover had lost weight, cut her hair and ditched the dull, shapeless clothing she had worn like a uniform. In the space of a few weeks, Elena had morphed from softly curved, bespectacled and repressively buttoned-down, into an exotically hot and sensuous swan.

Jaw clamped, Nick transferred his attention to the bride, Gemma O'Neill, as she stood beside his brother.

As the ceremony proceeded, Elena kept her attention fixed on the priest. Fascinated by her intention to utterly ignore him, Nick took the opportunity to study the newly sculpted contours of Elena's cheekbones, her shell-like lobes decorated with pink pearls and tiny pink jewels.

The sexily ruffled haircut seemed to sum up the changes Elena had made: less, but a whole lot more.

As Nick handed the ring to Gabriel, Elena's dark gaze clashed with his for a pulse-pounding moment. The starry, romantic softness he glimpsed died an instant death, replaced by the familiar professional blandness that made his jaw tighten.

The cool neutrality was distinctly at odds with the way Elena had used to look at him. It was light-years away from the ingenuous passion that had burned him from the inside out when they had made love.

A delicate, sophisticated perfume wafted around him. The tantalizing scent, like Elena's designer wardrobe, her new, sleek body shape and the ultramodern haircut—all clearly the product of a ruthless makeover artist—set him even more sensually on edge.

Gabriel turned to take the hand of the woman he had pledged to marry.

A flash of Elena's pink dress, as she bent down to whisper something to Sanchia, drew Nick's gaze, along with another tempting flash of cleavage.

With a brisk elegance that underlined the fact that the old Elena was long gone, she repositioned Sanchia next to Gemma. Nick clamped down on his impatience as the ceremony proceeded at a snail's pace.

Elena had been avoiding him for the past twenty-four hours, ever since she had arrived in Dolphin Bay. The one time he had managed to get her alone—last night to discuss meeting at the beach villa—she had successfully stonewalled him. Now his temper was on a slow burn. Whether she liked it or not, they would conclude their business this weekend.

Distantly, he registered that Gabriel was kissing his new bride. With grim patience, Nick waited out the signing of the register in the small, adjacent vestry.

As Gabriel swung his small daughter up into his arms, Elena's gaze, unexpectedly misty and soft, connected with his again, long enough for him to register two salient facts. The contact lenses with which she had replaced her trademark glasses were not the regular, transparent type. They were a dark chocolate brown that completely obliterated the usual, cheerful golden brown of her irises.

More importantly, despite her cool control and her

efforts to pretend that he didn't exist, he was aware in that moment that for Elena, he very palpably *did* exist.

Every muscle in his body tightened at the knowledge that despite her refusals to meet with him, despite the fact that every time they did meet they ended up arguing, Elena still wanted him.

With an effort of will, Nick kept his expression neutral as he signed as a witness to the ceremony. In a few minutes he would walk down the aisle with Elena on his arm. It was the window of opportunity he had planned for when he had arranged to change places with Kyle.

Negotiation was not his best talent; that was Gabriel's forte. Nick was more suited to the blunt, laconic cadences of construction sites. A world of black and white, where "yes" meant *yes* and "no" meant *no* and not some murky, frustrating shade in between.

As the music swelled and Elena looped her arm through his, the issue of retrieving an heirloom ring and unraveling the mystery of his father's link with Elena's aunt faded.

With Elena's delicately enticing perfume filling his nostrils again, Nick acknowledged that the only "yes" he really wanted from Elena was the one she had given him six years ago.

Elena steeled herself against the tiny electrical charge that coursed through her as she settled her palm lightly on Nick's arm.

Nick sent her another assessing glance. Despite her intention to be cool and distant and, as she'd done the previous evening, pretend that she didn't look a whole lot different than she had a month ago, Elena's pulse rate accelerated. Even though she knew she looked her very best, thanks to the efforts of the beauty spa, she was still adjusting to the changes. Having Nick Messena put her new look under a microscope, *and wondering if he liked what he saw,* was unexpectedly nerve-racking.

Nick bent his head close enough that she caught an intriguing whiff of his cologne. "Is that a tattoo on your shoulder?"

Elena stiffened at the blunt question and the hint of disapproval that went with it. "It's a transfer. I'm *thinking* about a tattoo."

There was a small tense silence. "You don't need it."

The flat statement made her bristle. "*I* think I need it and Giorgio thought it looked very good."

"Damn," he said softly. "Who is Giorgio?"

A small thrill went through her at the sudden, blinding thought that Nick was jealous, although she refused to allow herself to buy into that fantasy.

From what she knew personally and had read in magazines and tabloids, Nick Messena didn't have a jealous bone in his body. Most of his liaisons were so brief there was no time for an emotion as deep and powerful as jealousy to form. "Giorgio is…a friend."

She caught the barest hint of annoyance in his expression, and a small but satisfying surge of feminine power coursed through her at the decision not to disclose her true relationship with Giorgio. It was absolutely none of Nick's business that Giorgio was her personal beauty consultant.

In that moment she remembered Robert Corrado, another very new friend who had the potential to be much more. After just a couple of dates, it was too early to tell if Robert was poised to be the love of her life, but right now he was a touchstone she desperately needed.

Taking a deep breath, she tried to recall exactly what

Robert looked like as they followed Gabriel, Gemma and Sanchia down the aisle.

She felt Nick's gaze once again on her profile. "You've lost weight."

Her jaw clenched at the excruciating conversation opener. It was not the response she had envisaged, but all the same, a small renegade part of her was happy that he had noticed.

Her new hourglass shape constantly surprised her. The diet, combined with a rigorous exercise regime had produced a totally unexpected body. She still had curves, albeit more streamlined than they used to be, and they were now combined with a tiny waist.

She was still amazed that the loss of such a small amount of weight had made such a difference. If she had realized how little had stood between her and a totally new body, she would have opted for diet and exercise years ago. "Can't you come up with a better conversational opener than that?"

"Maybe I'm out of touch. What am I supposed to say?"

"According to a gossip columnist you're not in the least out of touch. If you want to make conversation, you could try concentrating on positives."

"I thought that was a positive." Nick frowned. "Which columnist?"

Elena drew a swift breath. After her unscheduled meeting with Nick in Auckland she had, by pure chance, read that he had dated a gorgeous model that same night. She said the name.

His expression cleared. "The story about Melanie."

"Melanie. Rhymes with Tiffany."

Nick's gaze sliced back to hers. "She's a friend of my sister, and it was a family dinner. There was no date. Have you managed to sell the villa yet?"

"Not yet, but I've received an offer, which I'm considering."

The muscles beneath her fingers tensed. She caught his flash of annoyance. "Whatever you've been offered, I'll top it by ten percent."

Elena stared ahead, keeping her gaze glued to the tulle of Gemma's veil. "I don't understand why you want the villa."

"It's beachfront. It's an investment I won't lose on, plus it seems to be the only way I can get you to agree to help me search for the ring."

"I've looked. It's not there."

"Did you check the attic?"

"I'm working my way through it. I haven't found anything yet, and I've searched through almost everything."

Her aunt had been a collector of all sorts of memorabilia. Elena had sorted through all the recent boxes, everything else she had opened lately was going back progressively in time.

There was a small, grim silence. "If you won't consider my purchase offer, will you let me have a look through before you sell?"

Her jaw set. "I can't see Aunt Katherine putting a valuable piece of jewelry in an attic."

"My father noted in a diary that he had given the ring to Katherine. You haven't found it anywhere else, which means it's entirely probable that it's in the house, somewhere."

Elena loosened her grip on the small bouquet she was holding. Nick's frustration that he wasn't getting what he wanted was palpable. Against all the odds, she had to fight a knee-jerk impulse to cave and offer to help him.

Determinedly, she crushed the old overgenerous Elena: *the doormat.*

According to Giorgio her fatal weakness was that she liked to please men. The reason she had rushed around and done so much for her Atraeus bosses was that it satisfied her need to be needed. She was substituting pleasing powerful men for a genuine love relationship in which she was entitled to receive care and nurturing.

The discovery had been life altering. On the strength of it, she intended to quit her job as a PA, because she figured that the temptation to revert to her old habit of rushing to please would be so ingrained it would be hard to resist. Instead, she planned to branch out in a new, more creative direction. Now that she'd come this far, she couldn't go back to being the old, downtrodden Elena.

Aware that Nick was waiting for an answer she crushed the impulse to say an outright yes. "I don't think you'll find anything, but since you're so insistent, I'm willing for you to come and have a look through the house for yourself."

"When? I'm flying out early tomorrow morning and I won't be back for a month."

In which time, if she accepted the offer she was considering, the villa could be sold. She frowned at the way Nick had neatly cornered her. "I suppose I could spare a couple of hours tonight. If I help you sort through the final trunks, one hour should do it."

"Done." Nick lifted a hand in brief acknowledgment of an elderly man Elena recognized as Mario Atraeus. Seated next to him was a gorgeous brunette, Eva Atraeus, Mario's adopted daughter.

Elena's hand tightened on Nick's arm in a weird, instant reflex. Nick's gaze clashed with hers. "What's wrong?"

"Nothing." She had just remembered a photograph she stumbled across a couple of months ago in a glossy women's magazine of Nick partnering Eva at a charity function. They had looked perfect together. Nick with his strong masculine good looks, Eva, with her olive skin and tawny hair, looking like an exotic flower by his side.

The music swelled to a crescendo as Gabriel and Gemma, with Sanchia in tow, stopped to greet an elderly matriarch of the Messena clan instead of leaving the church.

Pressed forward by people behind, Elena found herself impelled onto the front steps of the church, into a shower of confetti and rice.

A dark-haired young man wearing a checked shirt loomed out of the waiting crowd. He lifted a large camera and began snapping them as if they were the married couple. Embarrassment clutched at Elena. It wasn't the official photographer, which meant he was probably a journalist. "He's making a mistake."

Another wave of confetti had Nick tucking her in closer against his side. "A reporter making a mistake? It won't be the first time."

"Aren't you worried?"

"Not particularly."

A cluster of guests exiting the church jostled Elena, so that she found herself plastered against Nick's chest.

"I said I wasn't going to do this," he muttered.

A split second later his head dipped and his mouth came down on hers.

Four

Instead of pulling away as she should have, Elena froze, an odd feminine delight flowing through her at the softness of his mouth, the faint abrasion of his jaw. Nick's hands settled at her waist, steadying her against him as he angled his jaw and deepened the kiss.

She registered that Nick was aroused. For a dizzying moment time seemed to slow, stop, then an eruption of applause, a raft of excited comments and the motorized click of the reporter's camera brought her back to her senses.

Nick lifted his head. "We need to move."

His arm closed around her waist, urging her off the steps. At that moment Gemma and Gabriel appeared in the doors of the church, and the attention of the reporter and the guests shifted.

Someone clapped Nick on the shoulder. "For a minute there I thought I was attending the wrong wedding, but as soon as I recognized you I knew you couldn't be the groom."

Relieved by the distraction, Elena freed herself from Nick's hold and the haze of unscripted passion.

Nick half turned to shake hands with a large, tanned man wearing a sleek suit teamed with an Akubra hat, the Australian equivalent of a cowboy. "You know me, Nate. Married to the job."

Elena noticed that the young guy in the checked shirt who had been snapping photos had sidled close and seemed to be listening. Before she could decide whether he was lingering with deliberate intent or if it was sheer coincidence, Nick introduced her to Nate Cavendish.

As soon as Elena heard the name she recognized Cavendish as an Australian cattleman with a legendary reputation as one of the richest and most elusive bachelors in Australia.

Feeling flustered and unsettled, her mind still locked on Nick's statement that he was married to the job, she shook Nate's hand.

Nate gave her a curious look as if he found her familiar but couldn't quite place her. Not surprising, since she had bumped into him at Atraeus parties a couple of times in the past when she had been the "old" Elena. "You must be Nick's new girl."

"No," she said blandly. "I'm not that interested. Too busy shopping around."

Nick's gaze touched on hers, promising retribution. "It's what you might call an interesting arrangement."

Nate shook his head. "Sounds like she's got you on your knees."

Nick shrugged, his expression cooling as he noticed the journalist. "Another one bites the dust."

"That's for sure." Nate tipped his hat at Elena and

walked toward the guests clustered around Gabriel and Gemma.

Nick's gaze was glacially cold as he watched the reporter jog toward a car and drive away at speed.

Elena's stomach sank. After working years for the Atraeus family, she had an instinct about the press. The only reason the reporter was leaving was because he had a story.

Nick's palm landed in the small of her back. He moved her out of the way of the crowd as Gemma and Gabriel strolled toward their waiting limousine. But the effect that one small touch had on Elena was far from casual, zapping her straight back to the unsettling heat of the kiss.

Nick's brows jerked together as she instantly moved away from his touch. A split second later a vibrating sound distracted him.

Sliding his phone out of his pocket, he stepped a couple of paces away to answer the call.

While he conducted a discussion about closing some deal on a resort purchase, Elena struggled to compose herself as she watched the bridal car leave.

A second limousine slid into place. The one that would transport her, Nick and Kyle to the Dolphin Bay Resort for the wedding photographs.

Her stomach churned at the thought. There was no quick exit today. She would have to share the intimate space of the limousine with Nick then, sit with him at the reception.

Too late to wish she hadn't allowed that kiss or the conversation that had followed. Before today she would have said she didn't have a flirtatious bone in her body. But sometime between the altar and the church gate she had learned to flirt.

Because she was still fatally attracted to Nick.

Elena drew a breath and let it out slowly.

She should never have allowed Nick to kiss her.

Her only excuse was that she had been so distracted by Gemma finally getting her happy-ever-after ending that she had dropped her guard.

But Nick had just reminded her of exactly why she couldn't afford him in her life.

Nick Messena, like Nate Cavendish, was not husband material for one simple reason: no woman could ever compete with the excitement and challenge of his business.

Nick terminated his conversation and turned back to her, his gaze settling on her, narrowed and intent. "Looks like our ride is here."

Elena's heart thumped once, hard, as Nick's words spun her back to their conversation on the sidewalk in Auckland. The breath locked in her throat as she finally allowed the knowledge that Nick was genuinely attracted to her to sink in. More, that he had been attracted to her six years ago, *before* she had changed her appearance.

The knowledge that he had wanted her even when she had been a little overweight and frumpy was difficult to process. She was absolutely not like the normal run of his girlfriends. It meant that *he liked her for herself.*

The sudden blinding thought that, if she wanted, she could end the empty years of fruitless and boring dating and make love with Nick sent heat flooding through her.

Nick was making no bones about the fact that he wanted her—

"Are you good to go?"

Elena drew a deep breath and tried to slide back into her professional PA mode. But with Nick looming over her, a smudge of lipstick at the corner of his mouth, it was difficult to focus. "I am, but you're not."

Extracting a handkerchief from a small, secret pocket at the waist of her dress, she handed it to him. "You have lipstick on your mouth."

Taking the handkerchief, he wiped his mouth. "An occupational hazard at weddings."

When he attempted to give the handkerchief back, she forced a smile. "Keep it. I don't want it back."

The last thing she needed was a keepsake to remind her that she had been on the verge of making a second mistake.

Slipping the handkerchief into his trousers' pocket, he jerked his head in the direction of the limousine. "If you're ready, looks like the official photo shoot is about to begin." He sent her a quick, rueful grin. "Don't know about you, but it's not exactly my favorite pastime."

Elena dragged her gaze from Nick's and the killer charm that she absolutely did not want to be ensnared by. "I have no problem with having my photo taken."

Not since she had taken one of the intensive courses offered at the health spa. She had been styled and made up by professionals and taught how to angle her face and smile. After two intimidating hours beneath glaring lights, a camera pointed at her face, she had finally conquered her fear of the lens.

A good thirty minutes later, after posing for endless photographs while the guests sipped champagne and circulated in the grounds of the Dolphin Bay Resort, Elena found herself seated next to Nick at the reception.

Held in a large room, which had been festooned with white roses, glossy dark green foliage and trailing, fragrant jasmine, the wedding was the culmination of a romantic dream.

A further hour of speeches, champagne and exquisite food later, the orchestra struck a chord. Growing more tense by the second, Elena watched as Gabriel and Gemma took the floor. According to tradition she and Nick were up next.

Nick held out one large, tanned and scarred hand. "I think that's our cue."

Elena took his hand, tensing at the tingling heat of his touch, the faint abrasion of calluses gained on construction sites and while indulging his other passion: sailing.

One hand settled at her waist, drawing her in close at the first sweeping step of a waltz. Elena's breath hitched in her throat as her breasts brushed his chest. Stiffening slightly, she pulled back, although it was hard to enjoy dancing, which she loved, when maintaining a rigid distance.

Nick sent her a neutral glance. "You should relax."

Another couple who had just joined the general surge onto the floor danced too close and jostled her.

Nick frowned. "And that's why." With easy strength he pulled her closer.

Feeling a little breathless, Elena stared at the tough line of Nick's jaw and decided to stay there.

"That's better."

As Nick twirled her past Gabriel and Gemma, Elena tried to relax. Another hour and she could leave. Tension hit her again at that thought because she would be leaving with Nick, a scenario that ran a little too close to what had taken place six years ago. The music switched to a slower, steamier waltz.

Instead of releasing her, Nick continued to dance, keeping her close. "How long have you known Gemma?"

Heart pounding with the curious, humming excitement of being so close to Nick, Elena forced herself to concentrate on answering his question. "Since I started coming to Dolphin Bay for my vacations when I was seventeen."

"I remember seeing you on the beach."

Elena could feel her cheeks warming at the memory of just how much time she used to spend watching Nick on his surfboard or messing around on boats. "I used to read on the beach a lot."

"But not anymore?"

She steeled herself against the curiosity of his gaze, his sudden unnerving focus. "These days, I have other things to occupy my time."

He lifted a brow. "Let me guess—a gym membership."

"Fitness is important."

"So, what's behind the sudden transformation?"

Elena stiffened against the urge to blurt out that he had been the trigger. "I simply wanted to make the best of myself."

They danced beneath a huge, central chandelier, the light flowing across the strong planes and angles of Nick's face, highlighting the various nicks and scars.

He tucked her in a little closer for a turn. "I liked the color your eyes used to be. They were a pretty sherry brown, you shouldn't have changed that."

Elena blinked at the complete unexpectedness of his comment. "I didn't think you'd noticed."

No one else had, including herself. A little breathlessly she made a mental note to go back to clear contacts.

"And what about these?" he growled. His thumb brushed over one lobe then swept upward, tracing the curve of her ear, initiating a white-hot shimmer of heat.

He hooked coiling strands of hair behind one ear to further investigate, his breath washing over the curve of her neck, disarming her even further. "How many piercings?"

Despite her intense concentration on staying in step, Elena wobbled. When she corrected, she was close enough to Nick that she was now pressed lightly against his chest and his thighs brushed hers with every step. "One didn't seem to be enough, so I got three. On my lobes, that is."

His gaze sharpened. "There are piercings...else-where?"

Her heart thumped at the sudden intensity of his expression, the melting heat in his eyes. She swallowed, her mouth suddenly dry. "Just one. A navel piercing."

He was silent for a long, drawn-out moment, in which time the air seemed to thicken as the music took on a slower, slumberous rhythm. A tango.

Nick's hand tightened on her waist, drawing her infinitesimally closer. "Anything else I should know?"

She drew a quick, shallow breath as the heat from his big body closed around her. The passionate music, which she loved, throbbed, heightening her senses. Her nostrils seemed filled with his scent. The heat from his hand at her waist, his palm locked against hers, burned as if they were locked into some kind of electrical current.

She squashed the insane urge to sway a little closer. Wrong man, wrong place and a totally wrong time to road test this new direction in her life.

The whole point was to change her life, not repeat her old mistake.

Although, the heady thought that she could repeat it, if she wanted, made her mouth go dry. She hadn't missed the heat in Nick's gaze, or when he'd pulled her close, that he was semiaroused. "Only if you were my lover, which you're not."

"You've got a guy."

She frowned at the flat statement, the slight tightening of his hold. As if in some small way Nick considered that she belonged to him, which was ridiculous. "I date." Her chin came up. "I'm seeing someone at the moment."

His gaze narrowed with a mixture of disbelief and displeasure. "Who?"

A small startled thrill shot through her at the sudden notion that Nick didn't like it one little bit that there was a man in her life, even if the dating was still on a superficial level.

A little drunk on the rush of power that, in a room teeming with beautiful women, *she* was the center of his attention, she touched her tongue to her top lip. It was a gesture she became aware was an unconscious tease as his focus switched to her mouth.

Abruptly embarrassed, she closed her mouth and stared over Nick's shoulder at another pair of dancers whirling past. "You won't know him."

"Let me guess," he muttered. "Giorgio."

Elena blushed at the mistaken conclusion. A conclusion Nick had arrived at because she had deliberately failed to clarify who, exactly, Giorgio was. "Uh—actually, his name is Robert. Robert Corrado."

There was a stark silence. "You have *two* guys?"

She wasn't sure if the two tentative pecks on the mouth she had allowed, and which had been devoid of anything like the electrifying pleasure she had experienced when Nick kissed her, qualified Robert to be her *guy*. "Just the one."

Nick's gaze bored into hers, narrowed and glittering. "So Giorgio's past history?"

Elena tried to dampen down the addictive little charge of excitement that went through her at Nick's obvious displeasure. "Giorgio's my beauty consultant."

Nick muttered something short and succinct under his

breath. Another slow, gliding turn and they were outside on a shadowy patio with the light of the setting sun glowing through palm fronds and gleaming off a limpid pool.

Nick relinquished his hold, his jaw set, his gaze brooding and distinctly irritable. "Is Corrado the one you got the piercings for?"

The question, as if he had every right to expect an answer, made her world tilt again.

She had speculated before, but now she *knew*.

Nick was jealous.

Five

Elena dragged her gaze from Nick's and looked out past the pool and the palms to the ocean. Anything to stop the crazy pull of attraction and the dangerous knowledge that Nick really did want her.

The fact that he had been attracted to her before she had lost weight—that he actually liked her simply for who she was—was bad enough. But his brooding temper, as if the one night they had shared had somehow given him rights, was an undertow she wasn't sure she could resist. "Not that it's any of your business, but Robert doesn't care for piercings."

He definitely didn't know about the one she had gotten in her navel, or the pretty jeweled studs she had bought to go with her new selection of bikinis.

"So you didn't get the piercings for him."

The under note of satisfaction in Nick's voice, as if she had gotten the piercings for him, ruffled her even further. "I didn't get the piercings for *anyone.*"

But even as she said the words, her heart plummeted. She had tried to convince herself that the piercings were just a part of the process of change, a signpost that declared that she wasn't thirty—yet. But the stark reality was that she had gotten them because they were pretty and sexy and practically screamed that she was available. She had gotten them for Nick.

"You haven't slept with Corrado."

Annoyed at the way Nick had dismissed Robert, Elena stepped farther out onto the patio, neatly evading his gaze. "That's none of your business. Robert's a nice man." He was safe and controllable, as different from Nick as a tame tabby from a prowling tiger. "He's definitely not fixated on piercings."

"Ouch. That puts me in my place." Nick dragged at his tie. Strolling to the wrought iron railing that enclosed part of the patio, he pulled the tie off altogether, folded it and shoved it into his pocket.

Drawn to join him, even though she knew it was a mistake, Elena averted her gaze from the slice of brown flesh revealed by the buttons he had unfastened.

The balmy evening seemed to get hotter as she became aware that Nick was studying the studs in her ear and the tiny glimpse of the butterfly transfer. "I'm guessing from the pink earring that there's a pink jewel in your navel?"

The accuracy of his guess made her stiffen. The old adage "give him an inch and he'll take a mile" came back to haunt her. "You shouldn't flirt with me."

"Why not? It makes a change from arguing, and after tonight we may never see each other again."

Elena froze. The attraction that shimmered through her, keeping her breathless and on edge, winked out. She stared at the strong line of his jaw, the sexy hollows of his cheekbones, aware that, somehow, she had been silly enough, vulnerable enough, to allow Nick to slide through her defenses. To start buying into the notion that just because he found her attractive it meant *he* had changed.

The day Nick Messena changed his stripes she would grow wings and fly.

Lifting her chin, she met his gaze squarely. "*If* you find the ring." The instant the words were out, she wished she could recall them. They had sounded needy, as if she was looking for a way to hang on to him.

Nick glanced out over the pool, the sun turning the tawny streaks in his dark hair molten. "You make it sound like a quest. I'm not that romantic."

No, his focus was always relentlessly practical, which was what made him so successful in business.

Swallowing a sudden ache in her throat, Elena did what she should have done in the first place: she turned on her heel and walked back to the reception. As she strolled, Nick's presence behind her made her tense. By the time she reached her table he was close enough that he held her chair as she sat down.

He dropped into the seat beside her and poured ice water into her glass before filling his own.

Elena picked up the glass. The nice manners, which would have been soothing in another man, unsettled her even further. "If Aunt Katherine did receive the ring, then I guess all the gossip was true."

Nick sat back in his seat. "I don't want it to be true, either," he said quietly.

For a split second she was caught and held by the somberness of his expression.

A set of memories from her summers on the beach at Dolphin Bay flickered, of Nick yachting with his father.

It had usually been just the two of them, sailing, making repairs and cleaning the boat after a day out.

One thing had always been very obvious: that Nick had loved his father. Suddenly, his real agenda was very clear to Elena. He wasn't just searching for a valuable heirloom. He was doing something much more important: he was trying to make sense of the past. "You don't want to find the ring, do you?"

"Not if it meant an affair."

"You think they weren't having an affair?"

"I'm hoping there's another reason they spent time together."

Her stomach tightened at the knowledge that Nick was trying to clear his father, a process that would also clear her aunt. That despite his reputation there were depths to Nick that were honorable and true and *likable*.

That she and Nick shared something in common.

Elena watched as Nick drank, the muscles of his throat working smoothly. At that moment Gemma signaled to her.

Relieved at the interruption, Elena rose from her seat. She felt unsettled, electrified. Every time she thought she had Nick figured out, something changed, the ground shifting under her feet.

After a quick hug, Gemma stepped back. Almost instantly, she tossed the bouquet. Surprised, Elena caught the fragrant, trailing bunch of white roses, orchids and orange blossom.

Feeling embattled, she dipped her head and inhaled the delicious fragrance. Her throat closed up. After years of brisk practicality as a PA, she was on the verge of losing control and crying on the spot because she realized just how much she wanted what Gemma had: a happy ending with a man who truly, honorably loved her. "You should have given it to someone else."

Gemma frowned. "No way. You're my best friend and, just look at you, you're gorgeous. Men will be falling all over you." She gave her another hug. "I won't be happy until you're married. Who's that guy you're seeing in Sydney?"

Elena carefully avoided Gemma's gaze on the pretext that she was examining the faintly crushed flowers. "Robert."

Gemma grinned and hooked her arm through Gabriel's, snuggling into his side. "Then marry him. But only if you're in love."

Elena forced a smile. "Great idea. First he has to propose."

Elena walked back to her seat, clutching the bouquet. She was acutely aware that Nick, who was standing talking with a group of friends, had watched the exchange.

Gray-haired Marge Hamilton, an old character in Dolphin Bay, with a legendary reputation for gossip in a town that abounded with it, made a beeline for her. "Caught the bouquet I see. Clever girl."

"Actually, it was given to me—"

Marge's gaze narrowed, but there was a pleased glint in the speculation. "You'll be next down the aisle and, I must say, it's about time."

Elena's discomfort escalated. Nick was close enough that he could hear every word. But as embarrassing as the conversation was, she would never forget that, despite Marge's love of gossip, she had been fiercely supportive of her aunt when the scandal had erupted.

Elena dredged up a smile. "As a matter of fact, I'm working on it."

Marge's gaze swiveled to her left hand. A small frown

formed when she noted the third finger was bare. "Sounds like you have someone in mind. What's his name, dear?"

Elena's fingers tightened on the bouquet as she tried to make herself say Robert's name, but somehow she just couldn't seem to get it out. Something snapped at the base of the bouquet. There was a small clunk as a small plastic horseshoe, included for luck, dropped to the floor. "He's…from Sydney."

"Not that hot young Atraeus boy?" Marge sent a disapproving glance at Zane, who had flown in from Florida and happened to be leaning on the bar, a beer in his hand.

"*Zane?* He's my boss. No, his name is—"

Marge frowned. "At one point we thought you actually might snaffle one of those Atraeus boys. Although, any one of them is a wild handful."

Elena could feel herself stiffening at the idea that she was hunting for a husband in her workplace and, worse, the suggestion that the whole of Dolphin Bay was speculating on whether or not she could actually succeed. "I *work* for the Atraeus Group. It would be highly unprofessional to mix business—"

Nick's arm curved around her waist as casually as if they were a couple. His breath feathered her cheek, sending heat flooding through her.

"Were you about to say 'with pleasure'?"

Marge blinked as if she couldn't quite believe what she was witnessing. "I can see why you didn't want to say his name, dear. A little premature to announce it at a family wedding."

With surprising nimbleness she extracted a gleaming smartphone from her evening bag and snapped a picture. Beaming, she hurried off.

Elena disengaged herself from Nick's hold. "I was

about to say that it would be unprofessional to mix business with a *personal relationship*."

"Last I heard, personal relationships should be about pleasure."

"Commitment would be the quality I'd be looking for."

She noted Marge sharing the photo with one of her cronies. "The story will be all over town before the sun sets."

"That fast?"

"You better believe it. And, unfortunately, she has the picture to prove it."

"I must admit I didn't expect her to have a phone with a camera." Nick looked abashed.

Infuriatingly, it only made him look sexier. Elena had to steel herself against the almost irresistible impulse to smile back and forgive him, and forget that he hadn't responded to her probe about commitment. "Never underestimate a woman with a lilac rinse and a double string of pearls."

"Damn. Sorry, babe, it'll be a five-minute wonder—"

"Approximately the length of time your relationships last?" But, despite her knee-jerk attempt to freeze him out, Elena melted inside at the casual way Nick had called her "babe," as if they were intimately attached. As if she really were his girl.

Taking a deep breath, she forced herself to recall every magazine article or gossip columnist's piece she had ever read about Nick. And every one of the gorgeous girls with whom he'd been photographed.

Nick's expression sobered. "Okay, I guess I deserved that."

Elena set the gorgeous bouquet down on the table. "So, why did you do it?"

Nick's gaze was laced with impatience. "You should

ignore the gossips. They've had me married off a dozen times. I'm still single."

Elena pulled out her chair and sat down. She couldn't quite dredge up a light smile or a quip for the simple reason that a small, tender part of her didn't want there to be *any* gossip about her and Nick. The night she had spent with Nick, as disastrous as it was, had been an intensely private experience.

She didn't know if she would ever feel anything like it again. In six years she hadn't had so much as a glimmer of the searing, shimmering heat that had gripped her while she'd been in Nick's arms.

If people gossiped about them now, assuming they were sleeping together, that night would be sullied.

Nick frowned. "Is this about Robert?"

Elena almost made the mistake of saying *who?* "Robert isn't possessive." He hadn't had time to be, yet.

"A New Age guy."

She tried to focus on couples slow dancing to another dreamy waltz as Nick took the chair beside her. "What's so wrong with that?"

"Nothing, I guess, just so long as that's what you really want."

Elena's chest squeezed tight at the wording, which seemed to suggest that she had some kind of choice, between Robert and Nick.

Somehow, within the space of a few short hours the situation between them had gotten out of hand. She didn't think she could afford to be around Nick much longer. They needed to resolve the issue of the ring, and whatever else it was he was looking for, tonight.

She pushed to her feet again, so fast that her chair threatened to tip over.

Nick said something curt beneath his breath as he rose

to his feet and caught the chair in one smooth movement. In the process, her shoulder bumped his chest and the top of her head brushed his jaw.

He reached out to steady her, his fingers leaving an imprint of heat on her upper arm. Elena stiffened at her response to his touch, light as it was. She instantly moved away, disengaging.

Blinking a little at the strobing lights on the dance floor, and because her new contacts were starting to make her eyes feel dry and itchy, she collected the pink, beaded purse that went with her dress. "If you want to look for the ring, I'm ready now. The sooner we get this over and done with the better."

She was still clearly vulnerable when it came to Nick, but that just meant she had to work harder at being immune.

As she strolled with Nick out of the lavish resort, she tried to fill her mind with all of the positive, romantic things she could plan to do with Robert.

Intimate, candlelit dinners, walks on the beach, romantic nights spent together in the large bed she had recently installed in her Sydney apartment.

Unfortunately, every time she tried to picture Robert in her bed, tangled in her very expensive silk sheets, his features changed, becoming a little more hawkish and battered, his jaw solid, his gaze piercing.

Annoyed with the heated tension that reverberated through her at the thought of Nick naked and sprawled in her bed, she banished the disruptive image.

Six

Tension coursed through Nick as he walked through the resort foyer and down the front steps. Outside the sun had set, leaving a golden glow in the west. The air was still and balmy, the cool of evening infusing the air with a soft dampness.

"My car's this way." He indicated the resort's staff parking lot.

Elena paused beside his Jeep, which was parked in the manager's space. "No towing service in Dolphin Bay?"

"Not for a Messena."

She waited while he unlocked the Jeep. "I keep forgetting you're related to the Atraeus family. Nothing like a bit of nepotism."

He controlled the automatic desire to flirt back and held the door while Elena climbed in. As she did so, the flimsy skirt of her dress shimmied back, revealing elegant, shapely legs and the ultra-sexy high heels.

He found himself relaxing for the first time since Elena's pronouncement that she had a boyfriend. Although the hot pulse of jealousy that Elena had not only been ignoring his calls, but that sometime in the past few weeks she had started dating someone else, was still on a slow burn.

Robert Corrado. Grimly, he noted the name.

It was familiar, which meant he probably moved in business circles. Given that Elena was Zane's PA, she had probably met him in conjunction with her work for the Atraeus Group.

The thought that Corrado could be a businessman, and very likely wealthy, didn't please Nick. He would call his personnel manager and get him to run a check on Corrado first thing in the morning.

Jaw taut, he swung into the cab. The door closed with a thunk, and Elena's delicate, tantalizing perfume scented the air, making the enclosed space seem even smaller and more intimate.

The drive to the villa, with its steep bush-clad gullies and winding road, took a good fifteen minutes despite the fact that the property was literally next door to the resort, tucked into a small private curve of Dolphin Bay.

Security lights flicked on as he turned into the cypress-lined gravel drive. He checked out the for-sale sign and noted that it didn't have a Sold sticker across it yet.

Satisfaction eased some of his tension. He didn't need another property, and with its links to his father's past he shouldn't want this one. His offer to Elena had been a tactic, pure and simple, a sweetener to give him the opening he needed to research the past.

Although, once he had decided to make the purchase, the desire to own the property had taken on a life of its own.

On thinking it through, he had decided that his motives were impractical and self-centered. In buying the villa he hoped to somehow soothe over the past and cement a link with Elena.

Whichever way he looked at it, the whole concept was flawed. It presupposed that he wanted a relationship.

The second he brought the Jeep to a halt, Elena sent him a bright professional smile and unfastened her seat belt. "Let's get this over and done with."

With crisp movements, she opened her door and stepped out onto the drive.

Jaw tightening at the unsubtle hint that, far from being irresistibly attracted, Elena couldn't wait to get rid of him, Nick locked the Jeep.

He padded behind Elena, studying the smooth walls glowing a soft, inviting honey, the palms and lush plantings.

Elena was being difficult about the property, but he was certain he could bring her around. With the deal he was negotiating to buy a majority share in the Dolphin Bay Resort, in partnership with the Atraeus Group, it made sense to add the property to the resort's portfolio.

As Elena unlocked the front door, the sense of stepping back in time was so powerful that he almost reached out to pull her close. It was a blunt reminder that almost everything about a liaison with Elena had been wrong from the beginning, and six years on, nothing had changed.

The tabloids exaggerated his love life. Mostly he just dated because he liked female company and he liked to relax. If he wanted to take things further, it was a considered move with nothing left to chance, including the possibility that he might be drawn into any kind of commitment.

With Elena the situation had always been frustratingly

different; *she* was different. For a start, she had never set out to attract him.

Six years ago he had muscled in on her blind date because he had overheard a conversation in a café and gotten annoyed that her friend had set her up with a guy who could quite possibly be dangerous.

But, if he was honest, that had only been an excuse. Elena had been on the periphery of his life for years. She was obviously naive and tantalizingly sweet, and the idea that some other guy could date Elena and maybe make love to her had quite simply ticked him off.

She had been a virgin.

The moment he had logged that fact was still burned indelibly into his mind.

The maelstrom of emotions that had hit him had been fierce, but tempered by caution. At that point he'd had no room in his life for a relationship. His business had come first—he had been traveling constantly and working crazy hours. Elena had needed love, commitment, *marriage,* and he hadn't been in a position to offer her any of those things.

The accident and his father's death had slammed the lid on any further contact, but years later the pull of the attraction was just as powerful, just as frustrating.

Despite applying his usual logic—that no matter how hot the sex, a committed relationship didn't fit with his life—he still wanted Elena.

The fact that Elena wanted him despite all of the barriers she kept throwing up made every muscle in his body tighten. They were going to make love. He knew it, and he was certain, at some underlying level, so did she.

And now he was beginning to wonder if one night was going to be enough.

* * *

Elena stepped inside the villa and flicked on the hall light. Nick, tall and broad-shouldered behind her, instantly made the airy hall seem claustrophobic and cramped, triggering a vivid set of memories.

Nick closing the door six years ago and pulling her into his arms. The long passionate kiss, as if he couldn't get enough of her....

Elena's stomach tightened at the vivid replay. With one brisk step she reached the next series of light switches and flicked every one of them.

They didn't require that much light, since the boxes they needed to search were in the attic. She didn't care. With tension zinging through her, and Nick making no bones about the fact that he wouldn't be averse to repeating their one night together, she wasn't taking any risks.

The blazing lights illuminated the small sunroom to the left, the larger sitting room to the right and the stairs directly ahead.

Sending Nick a smile she was aware was overbright and strained, she started up the stairs. "Help yourself to a drink in the kitchen. I'll change and be right back."

There were four bedrooms upstairs. The doors to each were open, allowing air to circulate. Elena stepped inside the master bedroom she had claimed as her own. A room her aunt had refused to use and which was, incidentally, the same room she and Nick had shared six years ago.

With white walls and dramatic, midnight-dark floorboards, the bedroom was decorated in the typical Medinian style, with a four-poster dominating. Once a starkly romantic but empty testament to her aunt's lost love, Elena had worked hard to inject a little warmth.

Now, with its lush, piled cushions and rich pomegranate-red coverlet picked out in gold, the bed glowed like a warm, exotic nest. A lavish slice of paradise in an otherwise very simply furnished house.

Closing the door behind her, she began working on the line of silk-covered buttons that fastened the pink dress, her fingers fumbling in their haste.

As she hung the lavish cascade of silk and lace in her closet, her reflection, captured by an antique oval mirror on a stand, distracted her. In pink lingerie and high heels, her hair falling in soft waves around her face, jewels gleaming at her lobes and her navel, she looked like nothing so much as a high-priced courtesan.

Not a good thought to have when she was committed to spending the next two hours with Nick.

Dragging her gaze from an image she was still struggling to adjust to, she pulled on a summer dress in a rich shade of red.

Unfortunately the thin straps revealed the butterfly transfer on her shoulder. Maybe it was ridiculous, but she didn't want Nick to see the full extent of the fake tattoo. With all of the changes she had made, the addition of a tattoo now seemed like overkill and just a little desperate.

Unfastening the gorgeous pink heels, she slipped on a pair of comfortable red sandals that made the best of her spray-on tan, shrugged into a thin, black cardigan and walked downstairs.

When she entered the sitting room, she saw Nick's jacket tossed over the back of a chair. The French doors that led out to the garden were open, warm light spilling out onto a small patio.

As she flicked on another lamp, Nick stepped in out of the darkness, the scents of salt and sea flowing in with him. He half turned, locking the door behind him, and the simple, intimate motion of closing out the night made her heart squeeze tight.

With his jaw dark and stubbled, his shirt open at the throat, he looked rumpled and sexy and heartbreakingly like the young man she had used to daydream about on the beach.

Although the instant his cool, green gaze connected with hers that impression evaporated. "Are you ready?"

"Absolutely. This way." She started back up the stairs, her heart thumping faster as she registered Nick's tread behind her.

As she passed her bedroom, she noted that in her rush to get downstairs she had forgotten to close the door. The full weight of her decision to invite the *only* man she had a passionate past with to the scene of her seduction, hit home.

If she had been thinking straight she would have asked someone to come with them. A third person would have canceled out the tension and the angst.

Relieved when Nick didn't appear to notice her room or the exotic makeover she'd given the bed, she ascended another small flight of stairs. Pushing the door open into a small, airless attic, she switched on the light. Nick ducked underneath the low lintel and stepped inside.

He stared at the conglomeration of old furniture, trunks and boxes. "Did Katherine ever throw anything away?"

"Not that I've noticed. I suppose that if the ring is anywhere on the property, it'll be here."

As always when she thought of her aunt, Elena felt a sentimental softness and warmth. She knew Katherine had adored all of her nieces and nephews, but she and Elena had shared a special bond. She had often thought that had been because Katherine hadn't had children of her own.

Feeling stifled by the stale air and oppressive heat,

Elena walked to one end of the room to open a window. The sound of a corresponding click and a cooling flow of air told her that Nick had opened the window at the other end.

"Where do we start?" Nick picked up an ancient book, a dusty tome on Medinian history.

"Everything on that side of the room has been searched and sorted." She indicated a stack of trunks. "This is where we need to start."

"Cool. Sea trunks." Nick bent down to study one of the old leather trunks with their distinctive Medinian labeling. "When did these come out?"

"Probably in 1944. That's when the Lyon family immigrated to New Zealand."

"During the war, about the same time my family landed. I wonder if they traveled on the same ship."

"It's possible," Elena muttered. "Although, since your family owned the ships it was unlikely they would have socialized."

Nick flipped a trunk open. Another wave of dust rose in the air. "Let me get this right. My grandparents would have traveled first-class so they wouldn't have spoken to your relatives?"

Still feeling overheated, Elena ignored her longing to discard her cardigan. "The Lyons were market gardeners and domestic servants. They would have been on the lower decks."

With a muffled imprecation, Nick shrugged out of his tightly fitted waistcoat. Tossing it over the back of a chair, he unfastened another button on his shirt, revealing more brown, tanned skin.

Dragging her gaze from the way the shirt clung across his chest, Elena concentrated on her trunk, which was filled with yellowed, fragile magazines and newspapers.

Nick, by some painful coincidence, had opened a trunk filled with ancient women's foundation garments. He held up a pair of king-size knickers in heavy, serviceable cotton. "And the fact that some of them settled here in Dolphin Bay was just a coincidence, right?"

The tension sawing at her nerves morphed into annoyance. She had never paid any particular attention to her family's history of settlement, especially since her parents lived in Auckland. But now that Nick was pointing it out, the link seemed obvious. "Okay, so maybe they did meet."

Nick extracted a corset that appeared to rely on a network of small steel girders to control the hefty curves of one of her ancestors. "It was a little more than that. Pretty sure Katherine's grandparents worked for mine."

Elena vowed to burn the trunk, contents and all, at the earliest possible moment. "I suppose they could have been offered jobs."

He closed the lid on the evidence that past Lyon women had been sturdy, buxom specimens and pulled the lid off a tea chest. "So, maybe the Messena family aren't all monsters."

Feeling increasingly overheated and smothered by the cardigan, Elena discreetly undid the buttons and let it flap open. The neckline of her dress was scooped, revealing a hint of cleavage, but she would have to live with that. "I didn't say you were. Aunt Katherine liked working for your family."

The echoing silence that greeted her quiet comment, was a reminder of the cold rift that still existed between their families—the abyss that separated their lifestyles—and made her mood plummet.

Although she was fiercely glad she had ruined the camaraderie that had been building. Stuck in the confined space with Nick, the past linking them at every turn, she had needed the reminder.

Elena opened the trunk nearest her. A cloud of dust made her nose itch and her eyes feel even more irritated. She blinked to ease the burning sensation.

Too late to wish she'd taken the time to remove her colored contacts before she'd rejoined Nick.

Nick dumped an ancient bedpan, which looked like it had come out of the ark, on the floor. When she glanced at him, he caught her eye and lifted a brow, and the cool tension evaporated.

Suddenly irrationally happy, Elena tried to concentrate on her trunk, which appeared to be filled with items that might be found in a torturer's toolbox. She held up a pair of shackles that looked like restraints of some kind.

"Know what you're thinking." Nick grinned as he straightened, ducking his head to avoid the sloping ceiling. "They're not bondage." He closed the box of books he'd finished sorting through. "They're a piece of Medinian kitchen equipment, designed to hang hams in the pantry. We've got a set at home."

Elena replaced the shackles and tried not to melt at Nick's easy grin. She couldn't afford to slip back into the old addictive attraction. With just minutes to go before he was out of her life, now was not the time to soften.

She glanced at her watch, although her eyes were now watering enough that she had difficulty reading the dial.

"Are those contacts bothering you?"

"They're driving me nuts. I'll take them out when I go downstairs."

Once Nick was gone.

Nick closed the lid on the box with a snap that echoed through the night.

There was a moment of heavy silence in which the

tension that coiled between them pulled almost suffo-catingly tight.

"Damn," he said softly. "Why are you so intent on resisting me?"

Seven

The words seemed to reverberate through the room.

Elena glared at Nick. "What I don't get is *why* you want me?"

"I've wanted you for six years."

"I've barely seen you in six years."

Nick frowned as a gust of wind hit the side of the house. "I've been busy."

Building up a fortune and dating a long line of beautiful girls who never seemed to hold his interest for long… and avoiding her like the plague because she would have reminded him of *that* night.

And in that moment Elena acknowledged a truth she had been avoiding for weeks.

Now, just when she was on the point of getting free and clear, and at absolutely the wrong time—while they were alone together—it dawned on her that Nick was just as fatally attracted as she.

Outside it had started to rain, large droplets exploding on the roof.

Elena rubbed at her eyes, which was exactly the wrong thing to do, as one of the contacts dropped out. Muttering beneath her breath, she began to search, although with the dim lighting and with both eyes stinging, she didn't expect to find it.

Sound exploded as the rain turned tropically heavy. Moist air swirled through the open window.

She was suddenly aware that Nick was close beside her.

"Sit down, before the other one drops out."

"No. I need to find the lens, although it's probably lost forever." Added to that, her eyes were still watering, which meant her mascara was running.

Swiping at the damp skin beneath her eyes, Elena continued to search the dusty floorboards.

Something glittered, but when she reached for it, it turned out to be a loose bead. At that moment the wind gusted, flinging the window wide. Jumping to her feet, she grabbed at the latch and jammed it closed.

A corresponding bang informed her that Nick had closed the other window. As she double-checked the latch, Nick loomed behind her, reflected in the glass.

"Don't you ever listen?" The low, impatient timbre of his voice cut through the heavy drumming on the roof. His hands closed around her arms, burning through the thin, damp cotton of her cardigan. "You need to sit down."

Obediently, Elena sat on an ancient chair. Nick crouched in front of her, but even so he loomed large, his shoulders broad, his bronzed skin gleaming through the transparent dampness of his shirt. The piercing lightness of his eyes pinned her. "Hold still while I get the other lens out for you."

Elena inhaled, her nostrils filling with his heat and scent. Her stomach clenched on the now-familiar jolt of sensual tension. "I don't need help. All I need is a few minutes in the bathroom—"

Cupping her jaw with one large hand, he peered into her eyes. "And some drops."

Nick was close enough that she could study the translucence of his irises, the intriguing scar on his nose to her heart's content. "How would you know?" But she was suddenly close enough to see.

"I've worn contacts for years. Hold still."

As Nick bent close, his breath mingled with hers. She swallowed and tried not to remember the softness and heat of the kiss they'd shared on the steps of the church.

With a deft movement he secured the second contact on the tip of his forefinger.

Reaching into his pocket, he pulled out a small container of eyedrops and a tiny lens case. Setting the drops on the top of a nearby trunk he placed the lens gently in the case and snapped it closed.

Before he could bulldoze her into letting him put the drops in, Elena picked up the small plastic bottle and inserted a droplet of the cooling solution in each eye. The relief was instant. Blinking, she waited for her vision to clear.

Nick pressed the folded handkerchief she had given him earlier in the day into her hand. "It's almost clean."

"Thank you." Elena dabbed in the corners and beneath both eyes, then, feeling self-conscious, peeled out of the damp cardigan. "What else have you got in those pockets?"

"Don't ask."

Acutely aware that if Nick had another item in his pockets, it was probably a condom, Elena peered into a dusty mirror propped against the wall.

For a disorienting moment she was surprised by the way she looked, the tousled hair and exotic curve of her cheekbones, the pale lushness of her mouth.

She had definitely made outward changes, but inside she wasn't nearly as confident as that image would suggest.

Although according to Giorgio, that would change once she resurrected her sex life.

The thought that she could resume her sex life, here, now, if she wanted, made her heart pound and put her even more on edge.

An hour later, they emptied the final trunk. "That's it." Relief filled Elena as she closed the lid. "If the ring isn't here, then Katherine didn't receive it. I've already been through everything else."

"You searched all of the desks and bureaus downstairs?"

Elena wiped her hands off on a cloth. "Every cupboard and drawer."

Absently, she picked up a photo album, which she'd decided to take downstairs.

Picking up the cloth, she wiped the cover of the album. Glancing at the first page of photos, her interest was piqued. Unusually, many of the photos were of the Messena family.

She was aware of Nick's gaze fixing on the album. Somewhere in the recesses of her mind disparate pieces of information fused into a conclusion she should have arrived at a long time ago. Nick had taken a special interest in any photo album he had come across.

As she tucked the album under her arm and bent to retrieve her damp cardigan, a small bundle of letters dropped out from between the pages. Bending, she picked them up. The envelopes were plain, although of very good parchment, a rich cream that seemed to glow in the stark light. They were tied together with a white satin ribbon that shimmered with a pearlized sheen.

Her throat closed up. Love letters.

The top envelope was addressed to her aunt. Heart beating just a little faster, because she knew without doubt that she had found a remnant of the relationship her aunt had kept secret until she died, Elena turned the small bundle over.

The name Carlos Messena leaped out at her, and the final piece in the puzzle of just why her aunt and Stefano Messena had been personally linked fell into place. "Mystery solved," she said softly.

Nick tossed the cloth he'd used to wipe his hands with over the back of a broken chair. Stepping over a pile of old newspapers that were destined for the fire, he took the letters.

"Uncle Carlos," he said quietly, satisfaction edging his voice. "My father was the first son, he was the second. Carlos died on active duty overseas around thirty years ago. So that's why Dad gave Katherine the ring. It was traditionally given to the brides of the second son in the family. If Katherine and Carlos had married, it would have been hers."

With careful movements, he untied the faded ribbon and fanned the letters out on the top of a trunk, checking the dates on each letter.

Holding her breath, because to read the personal exchanges, even now, seemed an invasion of privacy, Elena picked up the first letter. It was written in a strong, slanting hand, and she was instantly drawn into the clear narrative of a love affair that had ended almost before it had begun, after just one night together.

Empathy held her in thrall as she was drawn into the brief affair that had ended abruptly when Carlos, a naval officer, had shipped out.

Elena refolded the letter and replaced it back in its envelope. Nick passed her the contents of the envelope he had just opened. On plainer, cheaper paper, it was written in a different hand. There was no love letter, but in some ways the content was even more personal: a short note, a black-and-white snapshot of a toddler, a birth certificate and adoption papers for a baby named Michael Carlos.

The mystery of Stefano's relationship with Katherine was finally solved: he had been helping her find the child she had adopted out. A Messena child.

Nick studied the address on the final envelope. "Emilia Ambrosi." He shook his head. "She's a distant cousin of the Pearl House Ambrosis. I could be wrong, but as far as I know she still lives on Medinos." He let out a breath. "Medinos was the one place we didn't look."

Elena dragged her attention from the sparse details of the Messena child. "You knew Aunt Katherine had had a baby?"

"It seemed possible, but we had no proof."

Feeling stunned at the secret her aunt had kept, she handed Nick the note, the snapshot and the birth certificate.

Gathering up the letters, she tied them together with the ribbon and braced herself for the fact that Nick would be gone in a matter of minutes.

She should be happy they had solved the mystery and found closure. Her aunt had tragically lost Carlos, but she had at least experienced the heights—she had been *loved.* They hadn't found the ring but, at a guess, Katherine had sent it to her son, who was probably a resident on Medinos.

Elena made her way downstairs to the second level. Placing the album and the sadly rumpled cardigan on a side dresser in the hall, she washed her hands and face, then waited out in the hall while Nick did the same.

Curious to see if Aunt Katherine had included any further shots of her small son in the album, she flipped to the first page. Unexpectedly, it was dotted with snapshots of the Messena children when they had been babies.

Nick's gaze touched on hers as he exited the bathroom, and the awareness that had vibrated between them in the attic sprang to life again.

She closed the album with a faint snap. "You must have suspected all along that a Medinian engagement ring, a family heirloom, was a strange gift for a mistress."

With his waistcoat hanging open, his shirt unfastened partway down his chest, the sleeves rolled up over muscular forearms, Nick looked tough and masculine and faintly dissolute in the narrow confines of the hall. "It wouldn't be my choice."

The thought that Nick obviously gave gifts to women he loved and appreciated ignited a familiar coal of old hurt and anger. After their night together she hadn't rated so much as a phone call.

"What would you choose? Roses? Dinner? A tropical holiday?"

She seemed to remember reading an exposé from a former PA of Nick's and her claims that she had organized a number of tropical holidays for some of his shorter, more fiery flings.

His expression turned wary. "I don't normally send gifts. Not when—"

"Great strategy." She smiled brightly. "Why encourage the current woman when there's always another one queuing up?"

There was a moment of heavy silence during which the humid, overwarm night seemed to close in, isolating them in the dimly lit hall.

Nick frowned. "Last I heard there is no queue."

Probably because he was never in one place long enough for the queue to form. Nick was more a girl-in-every-port kind of guy.

Elena found herself blurting out a piece of advice he probably didn't want to hear. "Maybe if you slowed down and stayed in one place for long enough there would be."

And suddenly Nick was so close she could feel the heat radiating off him, smell the clean scents of soap and aftershave, and an electrifying whiff of fresh sweat generated by the stuffy, overheated attic.

She stared at a pulse beating along the strong column of his throat. Sweat shouldn't be sexy, she thought a little desperately, but it suddenly, very palpably, was.

Nick's hand landed on the wall beside her head, subtly fencing her in. "With my schedule, commitment has never been viable."

"Then maybe you should take control of your schedule. Not," she amended hastily, "that I have any interest in a committed relationship with you. I have—Robert."

She didn't, not really, and the small lie made her go hot all over. But suddenly it seemed very important that she should have someone, that she shouldn't look like a total loser in the relationship stakes.

Nick's brows jerked together. "I'm glad we're clear on that point."

"Totally. Crystal clear." But her heart pounded at the edge in Nick's voice, as if he hadn't been entirely happy at her mention of Robert. Or that she had nixed the whole idea of a relationship with him.

Nick cupped her jaw, the heat of his fingers warm and slightly rough against her skin. "So this is just friendship?"

He dipped his head, slowly enough that she could avoid the kiss if she wanted.

A shaft of heat burned through her as he touched his mouth to hers. She could move away. One step and she could end the dizzying delight that was sweeping through her that maybe, just maybe, they had turned some kind of corner when they had uncovered the reason behind his father's relationship with her aunt.

That now that the past was resolved, a relationship between them wasn't so impossible.

Heart pounding as the kiss deepened, she lifted up on her toes, one hand curving over Nick's broad shoulder as she hung on. The tingling heat that flooded her, the notion that they could have a future, were all achingly addictive. She couldn't remember feeling so alive.

Except, maybe, six years ago.

That thought should have stopped her in her tracks. But the gap of time, the emotional desert she'd trudged through, *after Nick,* had taught her a salutary lesson.

She needed to be loved, and she absolutely did not want to remain alone. So far the search for a husband had proved anticlimactic. Good character and an appealing outward appearance just didn't seem to generate the "in love" part of the equation. Bluntly put, so far there had been no chemistry.

On the other hand, while Nick failed every sensible requirement, with him there was nothing *but* chemistry.

If she could have the chemistry and the committed relationship with Nick, she would be...happy.

His mouth lifted. He released her jaw as if he was reluctant to do so, as if he hadn't wanted the kiss to end, either.

Drawing a shaky breath, Elena relinquished her grip on Nick's shoulder.

A relationship with Nick? Maybe even with a view to marriage?

It was a major shift in her thinking. She didn't know if Nick could be anything to her beyond a fatal attraction. All she knew was that with his gaze fixed on hers and the unsettling awareness sizzling between them, the possibility seemed to float in the air.

That, and the knowledge that she was about to lose him in approximately two minutes.

She drew a swift breath. If she wanted Nick, she would have to take a risk. She would have to fight for him.

The fingers of her free hand curled into one of the lapels of his waistcoat where it hung open, her thumb automatically sweeping over the small button.

Surprise at the small possessive gesture flared in his gaze and was quickly replaced by a heat that took her breath. "I have to leave early in the morning."

She did her best to conceal her shock at how quickly he had cut to the chase and assumed that they would spend the night together, and the instant stab of hurt evoked by his blunt pronouncement that he had to leave. She had already known he was flying out on business. "Yes."

"You don't mind?"

She did, like crazy, but she wasn't about to let him know that. She had decided to take the risk of trying for a relationship with Nick. That meant she had to toughen up because a measure of hurt would naturally be involved.

She forced a smile. "I'm only here for a few days myself, then I need to be back in Sydney."

He wound a finger in her hair, the touch featherlight, and she tried not to love it too much. "For the record, my dating is usually on a casual basis. Most of it happens around yachting events when I'm racing."

That wasn't news to Elena. Her current Atraeus boss was a sailor, which meant there were quite often yachting magazines lying around in the office. Nick's name occasionally leaped out from the pages. "Which is quite often."

His breath wafted against her cheek, damp and warm and faintly scented with the champagne they'd drunk at the wedding. "Granted."

She inhaled and tried to drag her gaze from the slice of brown flesh and sprinkling of dark hair visible in the opening of his shirt. "But there have been a lot of women."

The album, which had been tucked under her arm, slipped and fell to the floor, as if to punctuate her statement.

His hands closed on the bare skin of her arms, his palms warm and faintly abrasive, sending darting rivulets of fire shimmering through her. "According to the tabloids. But we both know how reliable they are as a source of information."

Nick bent his head, bringing his mouth closer to hers. "If you don't want me to stay the night, just say so, and I'll leave you alone."

As he drew her close, she gripped the lapels of his shirt, preserving a small distance. Despite committing to a night with him, caution was kicking in. She needed more. "*Why* me?"

"For the same reason it's always been. I'm attracted to you. I like you."

A month ago, on a street in Auckland, he had said he

liked her. It wasn't enough, but coupled with the chemistry that vibrated between them and the fact that the rift between their families would now be healed, a relationship suddenly seemed viable.

Cupping Nick's stubbled jaw, she lifted up on her toes and kissed him. A split second later she found herself in his arms. With a heady sense of inevitability, she looped her arms around his neck, heat clenching low in her belly as she fitted herself even more closely against the hard angles and planes of his body.

After all the years of being calmly, methodically organized, of never losing her cool, there was something exhilarating about abandoning herself to a passionate interlude with Nick.

"That's better." He smiled, a glimpse of the uncomplicated charm that had always entrapped her, the kind of charm that made little kids flock around him and old ladies sit and chat. Except this time it was all for her and enticingly softer.

As Nick's mouth settled on hers, the reason he was so successful with women hit her. Despite the hard muscle and the wickedly hot exterior, he possessed a bedrock niceness that made women melt.

It was there in the way he noticed small things, like the color of her eyes and the fact that she was wearing contacts, the way he had rescued her from the blind date six years ago when he didn't have to get involved.

Her feet lost contact with the floor; the light of the hall faded to dim shadows as they stepped into a bedroom.

With a sense of inevitability, Elena noted the wide soft bed, with its lush piled cushions and rich red coverlet.

A lavish, traditional Medinian marriage bed, arrayed for a wedding. The room she had whimsically decorated.

The same room in which Nick had made love to her the last time.

Eight

Fitful moonlight shafted through a thick bridal veil of gauze festooning a tall sash window as Elena was set down on marble-smooth floorboards.

Nick shrugged out of his shirt, revealing sleekly powerful shoulders, a broad chest and washboard abs.

His mouth captured hers as he locked her against the furnace heat of his body. The hot shock of skin on skin momentarily made her head swim, but for all that, the kiss and the muscled hardness of his chest felt, oddly, like coming home.

Lifting up on her toes, she wound her arms around his neck and kissed him back. She felt the zipper of her dress glide down, the sudden looseness. Seconds later, she shrugged out of the straps and let the flimsy cotton float to the floor. Another long, drugging kiss and her bra was gone.

Bending, Nick took one breast into his mouth and for

long aching minutes the night seemed to slow, stop, as heat and sensation coiled tight.

She heard his rapid intake of breath. A split second later she found herself deposited on the silken-soft bed.

Feeling a little self-conscious and exposed, Elena slipped beneath the red coverlet, unexpected emotion catching in her throat as she watched Nick peel out of his trousers. She was used to seeing him in a modern setting as masculine, muscled and hot, but cloaked in moonlight and shadows, his bronzed skin gleaming in the glow of light from the hall, he was unexpectedly, fiercely beautiful, reminding her of paintings of Medinian warriors of old.

Dimly, she registered a rustling sound, like paper or foil. The bed depressed as Nick pulled the coverlet aside and came down beside her. The heat of his body sent a raw quiver through her as he pulled her close.

His gaze locked with hers, the softness she had noted in the hall giving her the reassurance she suddenly desperately needed.

He propped himself on one elbow, a frown creasing his brow. "Are you all right?"

She cupped his jaw and tried for a confident smile. "I'm fine."

One long finger stroked down her cheek. "Then why do I get the feeling that you're not quite comfortable with this?"

"Probably because I haven't done *this* in a while."

Something flared in his gaze. "How long?"

"Uh—around six years, I guess."

He said something soft beneath his breath. "Six years ago you slept with me."

The breath caught in her throat. "I guess, given what happened that night, you're not likely to forget."

"If the accident hadn't happened, I would still have remembered," he said quietly, "since you were a virgin."

For a split second she felt his indecision, the streak of masculine honor that had once been ingrained in Medinian culture. Abruptly afraid that he might abandon the whole idea of making love, that she might lose this chance to get him back in her life, she took a deep breath and boldly trailed a hand down his chest. "I'm not a virgin now."

He inhaled sharply and trapped her hand beneath his, then used it to pull her close so that she found herself half sprawled across his chest. "Good."

He rolled, taking her with him so that he was on top, his heavy weight pressing her down into the feather-soft mattress. Dipping his head, he kissed her mouth, her throat, and finally took one breast in his mouth.

Elena tensed, palms sliding across his shoulders, the sleek muscles of his back, as rivulets of fire seemed to spread out from that one point, culminating in a restless, aching throb.

He shifted his attention to her other breast, and in that moment heat and pleasure coiled and condensed, exploding into aching, shimmering pleasure as the night spun away.

Nick muttered something short and flat. Moments later his weight pressed her more deeply into the bed. She felt him between her legs, and relief flowed through her as slowly, achingly, he entered her.

The faint drag of what could only be a condom made her eyes fly open. The sound she had registered earlier suddenly made sense. Nick had sheathed himself, which meant he'd had the condom in his pocket.

The realization was like a cold dash of water. She shouldn't think about the condom. She shouldn't allow it to matter, but it did, because it meant he had been prepared to have sex with *someone,* not necessarily her.

Nick was oddly still, his expression taut as if he had gauged every one of the emotions that had just flitted across her face. "Something's wrong. Do you want me to stop?" A muscle pulsed along the side of his jaw. *"Yes, or no?"*

The words were quietly delivered, without any trace of frustration or need—just a simple question. Although she could see the effort it was costing him in the corded muscles of neck and shoulders.

The blunt, male way he had presented her with the choice brought her back to her original reason for making love: because she wanted another chance with him.

At the thought of losing him, contrarily, she wanted him with a fierce, no-holds-barred need that rocked her.

For every reason that shouldn't matter—because he was too elusive, too spoiled by the women he had dated and way too dangerous for her heart—he was the last man she could afford in her life.

And yet he was the only man to whom she had ever been truly, passionately attracted.

There was no logic to what she felt, no reason why he should smell and taste and *feel* right when no one else had ever come close.

Unless somehow, despite the frustration and anger and sheer loneliness of the past few years, she had somehow fallen for him, and he was *The One.*

She clamped down on the moment of shocked awareness. This was where she had gone wrong the first time with Nick—she had wanted too much, expected too much.

Every feminine instinct she had informed her that applying any form of pressure at this point would scare

Nick off, and she couldn't afford that. Framing his face
with her hands, she drew his mouth to hers, distracting
him from discovering that she might have done the one
thing that seemed to scare men the most and fallen for
him. "The answer is no, I don't want you to stop."

She promised herself she wouldn't cry as relief registered in his gaze and gently, slowly, he began to move.

There was a moment of utter stillness when he was
fully sheathed and they were finally, truly one, and then
he undid her completely by softly kissing her mouth.

His thumb brushed away a trickle of moisture that had
somehow escaped one eye, then he pulled her closer still,
holding her with exquisite care and tenderness as if he
truly did love her. A heated, stirring pleasure that was
still shatteringly familiar despite the passage of years,
gripped her as they began to move.

Locked together in the deep well of the night, the
angst and hurt of the past dissolved. Nothing mattered
but the way Nick held her, the way he made her feel,
as the coiling, burning intensity finally peaked and the
night spun away.

In the early hours of the morning, Elena woke, curled
in against the furnace heat of Nick's body. His arm was
curved around her waist, keeping her close, as if even in
sleep he couldn't bear to be parted from her.

A surge of pure joy went through her. She had taken
the risk, and it was working. Nick had been tender and
sweet, and the passion had, if anything, been even hotter, even more intense.

She was convinced that this time they really had a
chance.

The false start six years ago had muddied the waters,

but the hurts of the past shrank to insignificance compared with the happiness and pleasure ahead.

She smiled as she sank back into sleep. All was forgiven. She couldn't let the past matter when they were on the verge of discovering the once-in-a-lifetime love she was certain was their destiny.

A chiming sound pulled Elena out of a deep, dreamless sleep. She rolled, automatically reaching for Nick. The pillow where his head had lain was still indented and warm, but that side of the large, voluminous bed was empty.

Moonlight flowed through the window, illuminating the fact that Nick was pulling on clothes with the kind of quick efficiency that denoted he was in a hurry. Silvery light gleamed over one cheekbone and the strong line of his jaw as he glanced at his watch.

The bronzed gleam of broad shoulders and the strong line of his back disappeared as he shrugged into his shirt.

His gaze touched on hers as he buttoned the shirt with quick efficiency. "I have to leave now, otherwise I'll miss my flight out."

Elena jackknifed, dragging the sheet with her and wrapping it around her breasts. The memory of Nick explaining his schedule the previous evening flooded back. "The flight to Sydney."

The side of the bed depressed as he pulled on socks and shoes. "I have a series of business meetings I can't cancel. They're important."

"Of course." More important than exploring the passion they had found together, or the spellbinding sense that they were on the verge of discovering something special.

She drew an impeded breath and killed the idea of suggesting that, since she lived in Sydney and was due back soon, maybe she could go with him. It was too soon to put that kind of pressure on their relationship.

She needed to remember one of the rules Giorgio had given her about dating: that men liked to feel as if they were the hunter, even if that wasn't strictly the case.

She forced one of her professional smiles. "Of course. I understand completely."

His gaze was oddly neutral as he collected his phone from the bedside table and shoved it into his pocket. A trickle of unease made her stomach tighten.

As if he had already distanced himself from what they had done.

Bending, he picked something up from the floor. When he straightened, she recognized the packet of love letters. "I'll return these."

"No problem. I'm sure your mother will be relieved to know that Stefano was helping Katherine find her adopted child."

Another lightning glance at his watch, then Nick leaned across the bed and kissed her, the caress perfunctory. "Thanks. It was...special."

Elena froze. The awkwardness of the moment expanded when she failed to respond, but she had quite suddenly reached the end of her resources.

She recognized this part. Nick had gotten what he wanted: closure for the scandal that had hurt his family and another night of convenient passion. Now he was trying to step away from any suggestion of a relationship by leaving as quickly as possible.

Her fingers tightened on the beautiful sheets as Nick strode from the room. She heard his step on the stairs, then the sound of the front door quietly closing. A few seconds later, the rumble of the Jeep's engine broke the stillness of early morning.

She blinked back the burning heat behind her eyes and resolved not to cry. She could see why Nick's relationships ended so easily. He had concluded a night of passion in the same way he conducted his business affairs: briefly and with his gaze fixed on the next goal.

The full folly of returning to the scene of her last mistake and sleeping with Nick again settled in. Dragging the silk sheet with her, she wrapped it around herself and walked to the freestanding oval mirror. The moonlight was incredibly flattering. She was actually, finally, attractive in the way she had longed to be.

Although that hadn't seemed to matter to Nick. It hadn't tipped the balance and made him fall for her.

Which, she realized, was exactly what she had secretly hoped when she had started on the whole process of improving her appearance.

Admitting that pleasing Nick had been her motivation to change was painful, but if she wanted to move on she had to be honest.

She had been stuck in relationship limbo for years. Just when she was on the verge of forming a positive, rewarding romantic friendship with a nice man, she had thrown herself at Nick again.

Hitching the sheet up, she walked to the window and dragged the thick drape of white gauze back. A pale glow in the east indicated that the sun would soon be up. She needed to shower, get dressed and make a plan.

She had made the mistake of allowing Nick to get to her, again.

But the fledgling love affair that had dogged her for six years was finally finished. There would be no replays.

She was finally over Nick Messena.

Nick grimly suppressed a yawn as he sipped an espresso during his flight to Sydney.

Kyle, who was with him to represent the bank's interests in the partnership deal he was negotiating with the Atraeus Group, turned a page of his newspaper. "Did you find the ring?"

Nick took another sip of coffee and waited for the caffeine to kick in. "Not yet."

Briefly he filled Kyle in on the love letters and the adoption papers they had found, and that he had stopped by and spoken to their mother before he had left Dolphin Bay.

That had been a priority. The stark relief on Luisa Messena's face had told him just how much she had been holding out for the information.

There was a small vibrating silence, which finally broke through the grim flatness that had gripped Nick ever since he had driven away from Dolphin Bay.

Kyle put his newspaper down. "You and Elena looked like you were getting on. Last I heard, she wasn't returning your calls—"

"We found some common ground."

"Something's happened." Kyle's gaze had taken on the spooky, penetrating look that was a legacy of his time in the SAS, New Zealand's Special Forces. Something about Kyle's calm neutrality inspired respect and actual fear in the high-powered financial magicians he dealt with on a daily basis. When he turned up with the scary eyes the deal usually got done in minutes.

Kyle shook his head. "You slept with her again."

Nick's fingers tightened on his coffee cup. "I shouldn't have confided in you six years ago."

Kyle shrugged. "Dad had just died. You were understandably emotional."

Nick finished his coffee and set his cup down on the seat tray with a click. "According to the family, I have the emotions of a block of stone."

"Whatever. You've slept with Elena Lyon twice. That's…complicated."

Wrong word, Nick thought. There had been nothing complicated about what they had done or how he had felt.

He had been caught up in the same visceral hit of attraction that had captured him the night his father had died. An attraction that had become inextricably bound up with loss and grief, and what he had believed was his father's betrayal.

With the knowledge that his father and Katherine had not been involved, he should have been able to view Elena in the same way he viewed other past lovers. As an attractive, smart woman who was in his life for a period of time.

But the realization that Elena hadn't ever slept with anyone but him had sounded the kind of warning bells he couldn't ignore.

His reaction had been knee-jerk. As addictive as those hours with Elena had been, after years of carefully avoiding emotional entanglements and commitment, he'd found he couldn't do a sudden, convenient U-turn.

As much as he had wanted to spend more time with her or, even more crazily, take her with him, the whole idea of being that close to someone again had made him break out in a cold sweat.

Kyle signaled to a flight attendant that he wanted a

refill for his coffee. "If you don't want to talk about it, that's cool, but you might need to take a look at this."

Nick took the tabloid newspaper Kyle had been reading and stared at the piece written about Gabriel and Gemma's wedding. The details of the ceremony were correct, but it wasn't his brother and his new bride in the grainy black-and-white wedding photos.

Someone had made a mistake and inserted a photo of himself and Elena kissing on the steps of the church. It was flanked by a shot of him helping Elena into the limousine when they were on their way to have the official photos taken. A third snap as they had left the reception together rounded out the article. Apparently they were now on their way to a secret honeymoon destination.

A trolley halted beside his seat. A pretty flight attendant offered to take his cup. Absently, Nick handed it to her, barely noticing her smile or the fact that she was blonde, leggy and gorgeous.

According to the tabloids, *according to Elena,* the flight attendant was his type.

Although not anymore.

Now, it seemed, he had a thing for brunettes. Fiery brunettes with hourglass figures and issues.

Just as the flight attendant was about to move on, she glanced at the newspaper and sent him a brilliant smile. "I thought I recognized you. Congratulations on your marriage."

"Uh—I'm not actually married."

She looked confused. "That's not you?"

"It's him," Kyle supplied unhelpfully. "They've split up already."

There was a moment of shocked silence. The flight attendant dredged up a brilliant, professional smile that was cold enough to freeze water. "Would you like me to get you anything more, sir?"

The words, *like marriage guidance or an actual heart,* hung in the air.

"He's happy," Kyle supplied, along with the killer smile that usually made women go weak at the knees. "We have everything we need."

The attendant gave Kyle a stunned look, then walked quickly off, her trolley rattling.

Nick folded the newspaper and gave it back to Kyle. "Thanks for making her think that I ditched my wife of just a few hours because I decided to turn gay."

Kyle disappeared behind his paper again. "Look on the bright side. At least now she thinks *I'm* the villain."

Broodingly, Nick returned to thinking about the second night he had spent with Elena. Another passion-filled encounter that was proving to be just as frustratingly memorable and addictive as the first.

He hadn't been able to resist her and the result was that Elena had gotten hurt.

Nick retrieved an envelope from his briefcase and stared at the faded copy of the birth certificate and the photograph of the toddler he had brought with him.

He had found the reason his father had been in the car with Katherine the night they had both died. Not because Stefano Messena had been having an affair, but for a reason that fitted with his character. His father had been helping Katherine locate her baby.

The reason he had passed the ring to Katherine was because it, and a sizable chunk of the Messena fortune, belonged to his long-lost cousin. His birth year was the same as Nick's, which would mean Michael Ambrosi would be his age: twenty-nine.

An image of his father the last time he had seen him

alive flashed through Nick's mind. His chest went tight at the vivid picture of Stefano Messena tying down a sail on his yacht, his expression relaxed as he enjoyed the methodical process. It was the picture of a man who liked to do everything right.

For the first time he examined the fact that he hadn't been able to let anyone close since his father had died.

Intellectually, he knew what his real problem was, or *had been*. He had known it the moment he saw the love letters and birth certificate hidden in Katherine Lyon's photo album.

Because he and his father had been so close, no matter how hard he'd tried he hadn't been able to disconnect and move on. He'd stayed locked in a stubborn mind-set of grief and denial. The last thing he had wanted was to immerse himself in another relationship.

His mother and his sisters had probed and poked at his inability to "open up." The words *dysfunction* and *avoidance* had figured largely in those conversations.

Nick had stepped around the whole issue. Maybe it was a male thing, but he figured that when he felt like becoming involved in a relationship, he would.

But something had changed in him in the instant he had discovered the possibility that Stefano Messena hadn't cheated on or betrayed anyone.

Emotion had grabbed at his stomach, his chest, powerful enough that for long seconds he hadn't been able to breathe.

His fingers tightened on the birth certificate.

Grimly he allowed himself to remember that night. The time spent waiting for the ambulance, even though he'd known it had been too late. The hurt and anger that had gripped him at the way his father had died.

He knew now that his father had just been unlucky.

The heavy rain had made the road slippery. He'd probably been driving so late because he wanted to get home.

Home to the wife and family he loved.

He slipped the birth certificate and the photograph
back into the briefcase. The moment felt oddly symbolic.

Nick didn't personally care about the ring, which, in
any case, rightfully belonged to Michael Ambrosi. He
had what he wanted: he had his father back.

When they landed in Sydney the press was waiting in
the arrivals lounge.

Nick groaned and put on his game face.

Kyle grinned. "Want me to take point?"

"Just promise not to speak."

"Name, rank and serial number only. Scout's honor."

"That would have meant more about an hour ago on
the flight."

The questions, all centered on Elena, were predict-
able. Nick's reactions were not.

Instead of staying doggedly neutral, cold anger
gripped him every time a journalist directed another intrusive or smutty question at him.

By the time he reached the taxi rank he was close to
decking a couple of the tabloid hacks.

When they reached the Atraeus offices thirty minutes later, his normally nonexistent temper had cooled.
But his lack of control pointed up a change in himself
he hadn't expected.

Usually when he walked away from a liaison he felt
detached, his focus firmly on his next work project.

Right at that moment, he was having trouble concentrating on anything but Elena.

What she was doing and how she was feeling *about
him* was coming close to obsessing him.

The thought that she might actually get a tattoo or, worse, go back to the mysterious Robert, suddenly seemed a far more riveting issue than the resort package that would take his business portfolio to a new level.

As they stepped into an elevator, Nick took out his cell and put through a call to his PA, instigating a security check on Corrado. And, more importantly, requesting a full rundown on all of Corrado's business interests and a photo.

He hung up as the elevator doors opened up on the floor occupied by the Atraeus offices.

Constantine Atraeus, who was dealing with the negotiation himself, walked out and shook hands.

Constantine was both family and a friend. In his early thirties, he was incredibly wealthy, with a reputation for getting what he wanted. Although the powerful business persona was offset by a gorgeous, fascinatingly opinionated wife, Sienna, and now a cute young daughter.

Minutes later, with the deal on the table, Nick should have been over the moon. Instead, he found it difficult to focus. Kyle kept sending him questioning glances because it was taking him so long to read the paperwork.

A slim brunette with silky dark hair strolled into the room. Constantine's new legal brief. Apparently the last one had bitten the dust because he had tried to put a prenup on Sienna Atraeus. Sienna had seen him to the door, personally.

Nick forced himself to finish the clause he was reading, even though he knew he was going to have to go over it again because he hadn't understood a word.

The problem, he realized, was the legal brief. For a searing moment he had thought she was Elena, even though a second glance confirmed that she didn't look like Elena at all.

His gaze narrowed as he tracked her departure. His pulse was racing, his heart pounding as his inability to concentrate became clear.

He wanted Elena.

He wanted her back, in his arms and in his bed, which was a problem given that he had walked out on her that morning for the second time. If she ever spoke to him again, that in itself would be a miracle.

It had been difficult enough getting her to trust him the last time. The process had been slow and laborious. From the first phone call, it had taken weeks.

She had stood him up, refused his calls and done everything in her power to avoid him. He had managed to get close to her only through the good luck that his brother had gotten married to Elena's best friend.

If he wanted Elena back, he was going to have to engineer a situation that would give him the time he needed to convince her to give him another chance.

Two of his Atraeus cousins had employed kidnapping as a method of securing that quality time, although Nick didn't seriously think a kidnap situation would repair the rift with Elena. Both Constantine and Lucas had had long-standing relationships with their chosen brides, with the added bonus that love had been a powerful factor in each relationship.

It was a factor Nick could not rely on. He was certain that after a second one-night stand, Elena would no longer view him as a relationship prospect.

For a split second disorientation gripped him. He could kick himself for the mistake he'd made. He'd had Elena back in his arms, and then let her go.

He had further complicated the situation by leaving the field clear for Corrado.

If he wanted Elena back he was going to have to move

fast. Normal dating strategies wouldn't work; he was going to have to use the kind of logic he employed with business strategies.

With this new deal they would have a vital link in common: the Atraeus Group. He wouldn't exactly be her boss, but it would bring her into his orbit.

He'd had two chances with Elena and had blown them both.

He didn't know if he could create a third, but he had an edge he could exploit.

Try as she might, Elena couldn't hide the fact that she couldn't resist him.

Nine

Master of Seduction Meets His Match.

Elena stared in horror at the tabloid coverage of the wedding. She hadn't read many of the words; it was the image of the bride and groom that riveted her attention.

Someone had made a terrible mistake. A photo of her and Nick on the steps had been used instead of one of Gemma and Gabriel. The black-and-white print made her bridesmaid's dress look pale enough to be a bridal gown, and Nick looked the part with his morning suit. The shower of confetti and rice added the final touch.

There was nothing either scandalous or libelous about the brief article. If the photograph had been the correct one, it would have been perfectly nice, if boring, coverage of a high-end society wedding.

Acute embarrassment gripped her as she imagined the moment Nick saw the article and the photo, which portrayed the exact opposite of what he had wanted.

As wonderful as the night had been, something had gone wrong. They had been finished the moment Nick had walked out of the bedroom without a backward look.

She hadn't tried to cling to him, but that didn't alter the fact that watching Nick walk away a second time had hurt.

Or that in a single night she had been willing to sacrifice almost every part of her life to be with him, if only he had truly wanted her.

Elena snapped the paper closed. She could not be a victim again. She had changed her external appearance and now she needed to work hard at changing her actual life.

First up, she would take the new corporate position Constantine Atraeus had suggested she consider. With her executive PA skills, the psychology papers she had done at university and her recent experience of health and beauty spas, she was uniquely suited to reinvigorate the Atraeus spas.

She would be an executive, which suited her.

She was tired of catering to the whims of the megawealthy Atraeus bosses, who had appreciated her skills but who never really noticed her as a person.

A hum of excited possibility gave the future a rosy glow. She would probably need her own personal assistant, although that was a leap.

Two brief calls later, and her life was officially transformed.

Zane wasn't happy, since he had just gotten used to her taking care of every possible detail of his working day and travel arrangements. However, he was pragmatic. Since Elena had lost weight, his fiancée, Lilah, hadn't been entirely happy with her as a PA, much as she liked Elena. It was nothing personal, it was just that Lilah had a protective streak when it came to Zane.

"She might relax more after the wedding," Zane explained.

Elena hung up, a little dazed. She would never have believed it, but apparently she was now too pretty to be a PA.

She walked across to her hotel mirror and stared at her reflection. She looked pale and washed-out, but if Zane Atraeus said she was too pretty, then she was too pretty.

Nick had said she was beautiful.

She could feel herself melting inside at the memory of the way he had said those words, the deep timbre of his voice.

Jaw firming, she banished a memory that could only be termed needy and self-destructive.

Instead of going weak at the knees at any little hint of male appreciation from Nick, she needed to form an action plan. She needed rules.

Rule number one had to be: Do *not* get sucked back into Nick Messena's bed.

Rule number two was a repeat of the first.

She would make the rest up as she went along.

Critically, she studied the suit she was wearing. It was pink. She was over pink. The suit was also too feminine, too *pretty*.

She needed to edit her wardrobe and get rid of the ruffles and lace, anything that might possibly hint that she had once been a pushover.

From now on, red was going to be her favorite color.

She would also make a note to encourage Robert a little more. If she was in a proper relationship, it stood to reason that she would not be so vulnerable to a wolf like Nick Messena.

One month later, Elena opened her eyes as pads soaked in some delicately perfumed, astringent solution were removed from her now-refreshed eyes.

Yasmin, the head beauty therapist at the Atraeus Spa she had spent the past three weeks overhauling, smiled at her. "You can sit up now, and I'll start your nails. Can't have you looking anything less than perfectly groomed for your date. What was his name again?"

"Robert."

There was a small, polite silence. "Sounds like a ball of fire."

"He's steady and reliable. He's an accountant."

Yasmin wrinkled her pretty nose. "I've never dated one of those."

Elena reflected on the string of very pleasant dates she'd had with Robert. "He has a nice sense of humor."

Yasmin gave her a soothing smile as she selected a bottle of orchid-red nail polish and held it up. "That's important."

Elena nodded her approval of a color that normally she wouldn't have gone near. But with her transformation, suddenly reds and scarlets seemed to be her colors. Idly, she wondered what Nick would think of the nail polish.

She frowned and banished the thought.

Yasmin picked up one of Elena's hands and set to work on her cuticles. "So, tell me, what does Robert look like?"

Elena shifted her mind away from its stubborn propensity to dwell on Nick, and forced herself to concentrate on Robert. "He has green eyes and dark blond hair—"

Yasmin set one hand down and picked the other up. "Sounds a little like Nick Messena."

Except that Robert didn't have quite that piercing shade of green to his eyes, or the hot gold streaks in his hair. "Superficially."

"Well, if he looks anything like Nick Messena, he's got to be sexy."

"I wouldn't say Robert was sexy…exactly."

"What then?"

Elena watched as Yasmin perfectly and precisely painted a nail. "He's…nice. Clean-cut and extremely well-groomed. Medium build. He's definitely not pushy or ruthless."

Every attribute was the exact opposite of Nick's casual, hunky, killer charm. She had checked weeks ago before she had made the decision for a first date with Robert. After all, what was the point of repeating her mistake? She wanted a man who would be good for her. A man who would commit.

Yasmin painted another nail. "He sounds close to perfect."

"If there was a textbook definition for the perfect date, Robert would be it."

"Talking about perfect men, I saw a photo of Nick Messena in a magazine the other day." She shook her head. "I can't believe how *hot* he is. That broken nose… It shouldn't look good, but it is to *die* for."

Elena's jaw tightened against a fierce surge of jealousy. Swallowing, she tried to put a lid on the kind of primitive, unreasoning emotion that made her want to find the magazine Yasmin had been mooning over and confiscate it.

Jealousy meant she hadn't quite gotten Messena out of her system. It meant she still cared. "Why is it that a broken nose makes a guy more attractive?"

"Because he fights. Perfect men look like they're fresh out of the wrapper. Untried under pressure." She grinned. "I must admit, I like a guy who doesn't mind getting sweaty."

Elena blinked at the sudden image of Nick years ago when she'd walked past a construction site and glimpsed him with his shirt off, covered in dust and grease smears, a hard hat on his head. "I think we should talk about something else."

"Sure." Yasmin sent her a patient you're-the-client look.

The following day, after another pleasant date with Robert during which she had partnered him to one of his company dinners, Elena was packed and ready to fly back to New Zealand. She would spend a couple of days in Auckland, then travel on to Dolphin Bay where she was poised to add a new level of service to the resort business: a pamper weekend that included a relationship seminar she had designed herself.

Her stomach tightened a little as the taxi driver put her luggage into the trunk. Just because she was on her way back to Dolphin Bay didn't mean she would run into Nick. Chances were, he wouldn't even be in the country.

And even if he was, she had successfully avoided him for years. She could avoid him again.

He would get Elena back; it was just a matter of time.

Despite the fact that she had hung up on him again.

Broodingly, Nick placed his phone on the gleaming mahogany surface of his desk.

Not a good sign.

A familiar surge of frustration tightened every muscle in his body as he rose from his office chair, ignoring the cup of coffee steaming gently on his desk. Prowling to the French doors, he looked out over Dolphin Bay.

A heat haze hung on the horizon, melding sea and sky. Closer in, a small number of expensive yachts and launches floated on moorings, including his own yacht, *Saraband*.

Stepping out on the patio, he looked down over his new domain. He now owned a 51-percent share of the resort chain. It was a new turn in his business plan, but one that made sense with his close ties to the Atraeus family and their meshing interests.

Gripping the gleaming chrome rail, he surveyed the terraced levels of the resort complex. His eye was naturally drawn to gleaming turquoise pools below dotted with swimmers and fringed with cooling palms. Though it was the peaked roof of the villa in the adjacent curve of the bay that held his attention.

A hot flash of the night he'd spent with Elena blotted out the lavish tropical scene. The heat of the memory was followed by a replay of the hollow sensation that had gripped him when he had walked out of the villa just before sunrise.

His mother and his two sisters had read him the riot act about his dating regime a number of times.

He now no longer had the excuse of his father's so-called betrayal. As one of his sisters had pointed out, he was out of excuses. It was time he confronted his own reluctance to surrender to a relationship.

A tap on his office door jerked him out of his reverie. The door popped opened. Jenna, his new ultra-efficient PA, waved the file he had requested and placed it on his desk.

As he stepped back into the office, she sent him one of the bright, professional smiles that had begun to put his teeth on edge.

She paused at the door, her expression open and confident. "A group of us are going into town for lunch. You're welcome to join us if you'd like."

Nick dragged his gaze from the lure of the file, which he'd been waiting on. Absently he turned down the offer. Jenna was five-ten, slim and curvy in all the right places. He would have to be stone-cold dead not to notice that she was gorgeous in a quirky, cute way that would obsess a lot of men.

Although not him.

He should find her attractive. A couple of months ago, he would have. The red-haired receptionist in the lobby was also pretty, and a couple of the waitresses in the resort restaurant were stunning. The place was overrun with beautiful, available women, if only he was interested.

Opening the file, he began to skim read. Zane had given him a heads-up that a pamper weekend the Dolphin Bay Resort was scheduled to run in the next few days was Elena's pet project.

He was aware that she had quit her job as a PA and was now heading up a new department, developing the lucrative spa side of the resort business. The pamper weekend and seminar, designed for burned-out career women, was a pilot program she had designed and was entitled What Women Really Want: How to Get the Best Out of Your Life and Relationships.

His door opened again, but this time it was his twin sisters, Sophie and Francesca, who were home for a week's holiday.

They were identical twins, both gorgeous and outgoing with dark hair and dark eyes. Sophie tended to be calm and deceptively slow-moving with a legendary obsession with shoes, while Francesca was more flamboyant with a definite edge to her character.

Sophie, sleek in white jeans and a white tank, smiled. "We've come to take you out to lunch."

Francesca, looking exotic in a dress that was a rich shade of turquoise, made a beeline for his desk and perched on the edge, swinging one elegantly clad foot. "Mom's worried about you." She leaned over and filched his coffee. "Apparently you've gone cold turkey on dating for three months, and you're not sailing, either. She thinks you're sickening for something."

With the ease of long practice, he retrieved his coffee. "You'll have to try another tack. First of all, Mom isn't likely to worry when I'm doing exactly what she wants by not dating. And I've gone without dating for longer periods than three months before."

Sophie circled his desk and dropped into his chair. "When you were building your business and didn't have time for the fairer sex."

"News flash," Nick growled. "I'm still building the business."

Sophie picked up the file he'd dropped on the desk when he'd rescued his coffee and idly perused it. "But you have slowed down. Haven't you got some hotshot executive shark cutting deals and intimidating all of your subcontractors?"

Nick controlled the urge to remove the file from Sophie's grasp. "I've got a team of sharks. Ben Sabin is one of them."

Sophie looked arrested. "But you knew who I was talking about."

Nick frowned at Sophie's response to Ben Sabin, who had a reputation for being as tough on relationships as he was troubleshooting his jobs. He made a mental note to have a word with Sabin and make sure that he understood that Nick's sisters, both of them, were off-limits.

Francesca pushed off the edge of the desk, the movement impatient but graceful. "So what's up? Mom thinks you've fallen for someone and it isn't working out."

Nick dragged at his tie, suddenly feeling harassed and on edge. He should be used to the inquisition. His family was large and gregarious. They poked and pried into each other's lives, not because they were curious but because they genuinely cared.

As prying as his mother and his sisters could be, in an odd way he usually loved that they hassled him. He knew that if he ever got seriously messed with by a woman, they would be as territorial as a pack of wolves protecting their young.

Sophie frowned at the file. "Elena Lyon? Didn't you used to date her?"

Francesca's gaze sharpened. She strolled around the desk and peered at the file. "It was a blind date, only Nick wasn't blind. He set it up."

Nick frowned. "How do you *know* this stuff?"

Francesca looked surprised. "I used to study with Tara Smith who waited tables at the Dolphin Bay Coffee Shop. She overheard you telling Smale to find someone else to date and that if you ever heard he was trying to date Elena Lyon again, the next conversation would be outside, on the sidewalk." Francesca smiled. "Pretty sure that's verbatim. Tara's now a qualified accountant—she doesn't make mistakes."

Nick felt like pounding his head on the solid mahogany door of his office, but that would be a sign of weakness—something he couldn't afford around his sisters.

A small frown pleated Sophie's brow. "Elena was Gemma's bridesmaid, the girl in the picture when the tabloids mistakenly put the wrong photo in the paper."

Francesca went oddly still. "That would be the series of photos that fooled everyone into thinking Nick had gotten married."

There was a heavy silence as if a conclusion that only women could achieve had just been reached.

Sophie's expression morphed back to calm and serene. Nick groaned inside. He didn't know how they had connected the dots, but both of his twin sisters now knew exactly how interested he was in Elena Lyon.

Nick controlled another powerful urge to retrieve the file. If he did that, the inquisition would worsen.

Sophie turned another page, brow pleated, reminding him of nothing so much as a very glamorous, earnest female version of Sherlock Holmes. "Elena was the maid of honor at Gabriel's wedding." There was a significant pause. "Now she's coming back to Dolphin Bay for a weekend."

Francesca's gaze snapped to his. "Did she plan this?"

Nick's brows jerked together at the implication that Elena was scheming to trap him, when as of ten minutes ago she was still refusing to take his calls. "There is nothing planned about it. She doesn't know I'm here."

That was a mistake.

Nick pinched the bridge of his nose and tried to think, but something about the twin's double act interfered with normal brain function.

Francesca's look of horror sealed his fate. Five minutes ago he had been an object of careful examination and pity, but now he was a predator. It was strange how the conversations usually went that way.

Francesca fixed him with a fiery gaze. "If you're letting her come here and she doesn't know you own the hotel, well, that's…predatory."

Sophie ignored Francesca's outrage as she placed the file back on the desk and eyed him with the trademark calm authority that thirty years from now would probably be scaring grandkids. "Do you want her?"

In the quiet of the room the bald question was oddly shocking.

Nick's jaw clenched. As family inquisitions went, this one was over. "There is no relationship. Elena works for the Atraeus Group. She's coming to Dolphin Bay to work."

As far as he was concerned, technically, the relationship he was angling for would begin *after* Elena arrived.

An hour later, after a fraught lunch spent sidestepping further questions and a raft of romantic advice, Nick made it back to his desk.

Opening the file he'd been attempting to read earlier, he studied the letter that had come with the pamper weekend program. He would recognize Elena's elegant slanting signature anywhere.

Unfastening the pale pink sheet from the file fastener, he lifted it to his nostrils. The faint exotic scent of lilies assailed him, laced with a musky under note that set him sensually on edge.

Loosening his tie, he sat back in his seat and studied Elena's pamper weekend package. Though designed for women, men were welcome to attend.

He flicked through the pages until he arrived at a quiz. Gaze sharpening, he studied a sheet of multiple-choice questions entitled The Love Test.

The stated object of the quiz, one of the few elements of the package aimed at men, was to find out if the man in a woman's life knew how to really and truly love and appreciate her.

He flicked through the pages, twenty questions in all that ignored the more commonly perceived signs of a good relationship, such as flowers, gifts and dating. Instead the quiz wound through a psychological minefield, dealing with issues such as emotional honesty, the ability to understand a woman's needs, and with commitment.

As far as Nick could make out, the quiz didn't focus on what a man could aspire to romantically so much as highlight the age-old masculine traits that would make him stumble.

The question on when a relationship should be consummated was a case in point. For most men the answer to that question was simple. Sex was a priority, because in a man's mind until he had made a woman his completely, there was an element of uncertainty that didn't sit well with the male psyche.

Setting the test sheets down, he turned to the answers, frowning as he read through. The questions he had taken a guess at were all wrong.

As far as he could make out, no ordinary man could hope to score well. It would take an intellectual studying psychology or some kind of New Age paragon.

Like Robert Corrado.

His jaw tightened. From the few comments Elena had made, if Robert took the test, he would pass with flying colors. From the research Nick had done on Corrado, he was inclined to agree.

His fingers tightened on the page, crumpling it. As highly as he was certain Robert would score, he didn't think he was the kind of man to make a woman like Elena happy. She would be bored with him in a matter of months. Elena needed a man who wouldn't be intimidated by her formidable strength of character, her passionate intensity.

Nick was that man.

The moment was defining.

He straightened out the page of answers and reattached it to the file. Over the years, commitment had not been a part of any of his relationships.

But now, with the expansion of his business, and several highly paid executives taking the lion's share of the work, he didn't have quite so much to do.

He had time on his hands. And, as luck or fate would have it, once again Elena Lyon was in his equation.

And he was on the brink of losing her to another man.

In that moment, an internal tension he hadn't known existed relaxed, and the focused, masculine drive to attain and hold on to the woman he wanted, that had been missing for so many years, settled smoothly into place.

Six years had passed. Years in which Elena had been single and free, prey to any male who cared to claim her.

But not anymore.

Elena was his. He had hurt her—twice—but there was no way he was going to tamely stand aside and give Corrado a chance at her.

His resolve firmly in place, he checked the answer sheets to find the highest-scoring answers for each question. His frown increased as he read. Out of a possible score of sixty, with a couple of lucky guesses thrown in, he might have made five points. If that wasn't bad enough, the grading system, at odds with the smooth New Age language, was punitive. Thirty points, a pass in any man's language, was considered to be "indifferent." Ten points was "extremely poor." At five points he balanced on the cusp of "disastrous" and "a relationship mistake of catastrophic proportions."

Irritation coursed through him. There was no possibility that any red-blooded male could score well. But information was power and if he wasn't mistaken, he had just been given the key to getting Elena back.

The pamper weekend and the seminar provided the window of opportunity he needed.

Setting the sheet of answers back on top of the file, he walked through to the next office. He offered Alex Ridley, the hotel manager, a well-earned few days off, during which time he would manage the resort. An hour later, he had cleared his schedule for those three days.

Elena wouldn't be happy when she arrived and found him in residence, but he would cope with that hurdle when they got to it.

After the way he had messed up, he was well aware that negotiation wouldn't work. With the skills Elena had honed during her years as a personal assistant to his Atraeus cousins, she would ruthlessly cut him off. Desperate measures were required.

Picking up the quiz, he broodingly read through the questions again.

He didn't know if he would ever be in a position to do the quiz, but at this juncture he needed to be prepared for any eventuality. Picking up a pen, he systematically ticked the correct answer for each question. The 100-percent score entitled him to encircle the grade that assured him he was A Perfect Relationship Partner.

It was cheating.

But as far as he was concerned, when it came to getting Elena back, all was fair in love and war.

Ten

Elena crossed Dolphin Bay's county line just minutes
short of midnight. The Dolphin Bay sign was briefly illuminated in the wash of headlights as she changed down
for a curve and braked. The familiar arching entrance to
the Messena Estate loomed, and her heart beat a brief,
unwelcome tattoo in her chest.

She had to stop thinking about Nick. By now he would
be thousands of miles away, probably on some sand-
blasted site in Dubai and doing what was closest to his
heart: making millions.

A tight corner loomed. She slowed even further as she
drove through a bush reserve, the road slick with recent
rain and the moonlight blocked by large, dripping ponga
ferns arching over the road.

The massive plastered gateposts of the resort glowed
softly ahead. Relieved, she turned onto the smoothly
sealed resort road and accelerated, climbing steadily.

The lush rainforest gave way to reveal a breathtaking expanse of moonlit sea. Nestled amidst bush-clad hills and framed by the shimmering backdrop of the Pacific Ocean, the resort glittered, patently luxurious and very, very private.

Minutes later, she drew up outside a security gate.

The resort boasted a conference center, a world-class private golf course, a marina and a helipad. They catered to the luxury end of the market and were open for business 24/7, but for security reasons—mostly centered around the extremely wealthy clientele who stayed there and their privacy needs—the gates were locked from midnight until six in the morning.

Guest were issued key cards in advance, but weirdly, her key card envelope, which had been couriered to her, had been empty. Since she didn't yet have a card, on arrival she had to ring the reception desk so they could dispatch someone to unlock the gate and let her in. It all seemed unacceptably low-tech to Elena. She had already sent a very short email to the manager informing him that he needed to lift his game in this respect.

Once she checked in, apparently she would be issued a key card and could come and go as she pleased.

Jaw locked, she pushed the door open, climbed out into the balmy night and took a moment to stretch the kinks out. Just a few yards away, water lapped on honey-colored sand, the soothing rhythm underpinned by an onshore breeze flowing through the pohutukawa trees that overhung parts of the beach. During daylight hours, the stunning red blooms would provide a brilliant contrast to the intense blue of sea and sky.

She examined the fortresslike wrought iron gates, searching for the intercom. A small red light winked off to one side. Seconds later a receptionist with a smooth, warm voice answered her and assured her that someone would unlock the gate for her shortly.

Tiredness washed through Elena as she strolled across the short patch of perfectly mown grass that separated the driveway from the beach. Peeling out of her strappy red high heels, she stepped down onto the sand.

It was close on high tide. Letting her shoes dangle from her fingers, she walked a few steps until she was ankle deep in the creamy wash of the waves, drawn by the sheer romantic beauty of the moon suspended over the water.

The throaty rumble of an engine broke the soothing moment. Reluctantly, she retraced her steps. Powerful headlights speared the murky darkness, pinning her. The SUV, which was black and glossy with expensive, chunky lines, came to a smooth halt behind the wrought iron gates, the engine idling.

The driver didn't immediately climb out. Frustrated, she attempted to identify who it was behind the wheel, but the glaring halogen headlights had killed her night vision. A peculiar sense of premonition tightened low in her belly.

The door swung open. A broad-shouldered figure swung smoothly out from behind the wheel and the premonition coalesced into knowledge.

Despite the fact that she was braced for the reaction, her stomach plunged. Dressed in faded jeans and designer trainers, a soft muscle T-shirt molding the contours of his chest and leaving tanned biceps bare, Nick looked as tall, dark and dangerous as the last time she had seen him, *naked and in her bed.*

She went hot, then cold, then hot again. A weird pastiche of emotions seized her: embarrassment, dismay, a familiar sharp awareness, a jolt of old fury.

He gave her a lightning-fast once-over, making her aware of the messy strands of hair blowing around her cheeks and her sand-covered feet. Despite the fact that she was dressed for work in a tailored gray suit, she suddenly felt underdressed.

"Nick." She reached for the smooth professionalism that went with the suit, the elegant shoes and her new executive status. "This is a surprise."

And his presence threw some light on the resort's failure to supply her with a key card. Obviously, for some reason of his own, Nick had wanted another conversation.

His gaze, between the bars, was considering. "Not my fault. You didn't return my calls."

Two phone calls, four weeks and two days out? After she had been dumped—*for the second time*—by a man who had a reputation for running through women?

She held on to her temper with difficulty. "Sorry. I've been a little busy lately."

"You've cut your hair."

"It was time for a change."

A whole lot of changes. The feathery, pixie cut went well with her new executive job. Plus, the new, sharper style made her feel that she was moving on emotionally.

His gaze was distant as he depressed a remote for the gate and she wondered if she'd imagined the initial flash of masculine interest.

With careful precision, she deposited the red shoes on the passenger seat of her car. "What are you doing here?"

The weird sense of premonition that had gripped her was back. In none of her contacts with the Dolphin Bay Resort had Nick's name been mentioned. He wasn't listed on the website or in any of the correspondence she'd received from the resort when she had set up the seminar. "Tell me you're a guest."

Although, he couldn't be a guest. His family's enormous luxury house was just up the road and guests didn't open gates.

His gaze connected with hers, sending chills zinging down her spine again, and the brief fantasy that this was just as much of a surprise to Nick as it was to her evaporated. He had been expecting her.

"I'm not a guest. Haven't you heard? As of two days ago, I'm a part owner of the Dolphin Bay Resort."

Elena parked her car outside the reception area. She was now officially in shock.

Although maybe she should have seen this coming. She knew Nick had been working on some deal at Gabriel and Gemma's wedding. She just hadn't put it together with the news that the Atraeus family were shifting shares around within the family.

She had assumed that an Atraeus would take over the New Zealand side of the resort business. She had forgotten that Nick Messena was an Atraeus on his mother's side.

Nick insisted on helping her with her bags, then waited while she checked in at the reception desk. The owner of the smooth voice was a tall redhead with a spectacular figure and a pleasant manner. Once Elena had signed the register and obtained a site map of the resort, she looped the strap of her handbag over her shoulder, picked up her briefcase and reached for her overnight suitcase. Nick beat her to it.

"I'll show you to your cottage."

"I have a map. I can find my own way."

"It's no problem. All part of the service."

Briefly, she considered trying to wrestle the case back then, gave up on the notion and reluctantly followed Nick as he stepped back out into the night. The resort wasn't a high-rise complex—it comprised a number of layers of apartments and cottages, each set in their own lushly landscaped areas to preserve privacy. Her cottage was located in sector C. According to the map, it couldn't be more than one hundred yards away.

As she strolled, she kept an eye on the curving path, which had narrowed, meaning that she had to move closer to Nick.

In her eagerness to keep distance between them, one of her heels slipped off the edge and sank into a thick layer of shells. His hand landed in the small of her back, steadying her. She stiffened, moving away from the heat of his palm, careful not to stumble again.

He indicated a branching pathway and an attractive hardwood building nestled among palms. A tinkling fountain was positioned to one side.

Seconds later, relieved, she slid her key card into the lock and opened her door. Soft light automatically filled the small, inviting hallway. She set her handbag and her briefcase down on the exquisite hardwood floors and turned to collect her case.

Moonlight glinted on the tough line of Nick's jaw. "Now that you're here,' he said with a smooth confidence that set her teeth on edge, "we can finally talk."

"It's late. And this conversation was over a long time ago." If memory served her correctly, it had involved three words and the last one had been "special."

His jaw tightened, the first kink in his composure

she'd seen so far, and suddenly the ball was back in her part of the court.

He set the case down. "I know I behaved badly last month, but I was hoping we could—"

"What, Nick?" She checked her watch, anything to take her mind off the riveting notion that Nick was working up to doing the one thing she had wanted when she had woken up after their night together. He was on the verge of suggesting they spend some time together.

The luminous dial indicated it was almost one in the morning.

He stepped a little closer. The wash of golden light from the porch of her cottage gleamed off his mouthwatering cheekbones. "Since you're here for the weekend I was hoping we could spend some time together." Startled that he had actually said the words, she dragged her gaze from the odd diffidence of his. It occurred to her that he seemed sorry that he had hurt her. As if he really did want—

She forced herself to edit that line of thought. This was Nick. She would not be fooled again.

Taking a deep breath, she dismissed the old, automatic desire to soften, to do exactly what *he* wanted. "I can't think why."

"Because I want another chance with you."

The words were flatly stated, and they sent an electrifying thrill through her. For a split second she was riveted to the spot, quite frankly stunned, then she pulled herself up short. "When did you decide this?"

"A month ago."

She blinked. "I don't believe you."

He shrugged. "It's the truth."

His gaze dropped to her mouth.

Did he actually want to kiss her?

She should be furious, but for the first time in years, armed by hurt, she felt in control of her emotions and entirely capable of resisting him.

Heart pounding, high on an addictive, giddy sense of victory, she held her ground. "I don't understand why."

"This is why." He stepped closer, filling the doorway, his gaze fastened on hers and, like a switch flicking on, her whole body was suddenly alive and humming.

Nick's breath wafted against her cheek, warm and laced with the faintest hint of coffee. After a month of misery and platonic dating, the thought of kissing Nick Messena should leave her utterly cold. Unfortunately, it didn't.

"Thanks for carrying my bag." With a deliberate motion, Elena took a half step back into the hall, closed the door and leaned back on it. Her heart was pounding out of control. She felt weird and slightly feverish, and there it was. Her problem.

Nick Messena, unfortunately, still qualified as a fatal attraction. Close to irresistible and very, very bad for her.

Just like the last time, he was making no bones about the fact that he wanted her, and that in itself was very seductive.

But touching Nick Messena, kissing him—doing anything at all with him—was crazy. He was the boyfriend no self-respecting woman should allow herself to have... except in her fantasies.

She touched her lips, which felt sensitive and tender, even though she hadn't been kissed.

So, okay...Nick Messena still affected her, but she was almost certain that for him there was little or no emotion involved.

He was all about the chase. Commitment was not his middle name.

But after what had happened the last time they had met, it was definitely hers.

Nick's pulse settled into a steady beat as he walked to his own cottage, which was situated next door to Elena's.

The encounter hadn't gone well, but he had been braced for that.

He'd made love to her and left her—twice. He was going to have a tough time reclaiming her trust.

His pulse picked up a notch as he glimpsed Elena, just visible through the wide glass doors in her sitting room, easing slim, delicately arched feet out of her shoes.

With the addition of the red shoes, the gray suit, which could have been dull and businesslike, was cutting-edge and outrageously sexy.

He watched as she walked into the kitchenette, her stride measured, her spine straight, before she finally disappeared from view. It was an award-winning act, but no amount of control could completely repress the sleek, feminine sway to her hips or the fire he knew was stored behind those guarded eyes.

The red shoes said it all. The passion was still there.

He had made a mistake in leaving her. He should have kept her with him, but it was too late to turn the clock back now.

On the plus side, he finally had her back in his territory. He had three days, and the clock was ticking.

Unlocking his door, he stepped inside and walked through to his shower. Now all he had to do was convince her that the chemistry that exploded between them was worth another try. She hadn't let him kiss her, but it had been close.

Satisfaction eased some of his tension as he peeled out of his clothing and stepped beneath twin jets of cool water.

The night hadn't been a complete washout.

Despite the fact that she had closed the door in his face, he was certain that Elena Lyon still wanted him.

Eleven

The next morning, Elena dressed with care for the official part of the program: the What Women Really Want seminar.

Keeping her mind firmly off the fact that, despite everything, she was still attracted to Nick, she studied the filmy pink-and-orange halter top and white resort-style pants. The hot, tropical colors of the top revealed her smooth golden tan and a hint of cleavage. The pants clung to her hips and floated around her ankles, making the most of her new figure.

The outfit was perfect for a luxury resort, but even so she was tempted to retreat behind the business persona that had been her protective armor for years. Picking up pretty pink-and-gold earrings, she determinedly fitted them to her lobes.

The sound of a door closing in the cottage next door distracted her. A glimpse of Nick, dressed in narrow dark pants and a dark polo, strolling in the direction of the resort, made her heart slam against the wall of her chest.

The path he was using was the same one that led to her cottage and one other. Since she had heard a door close and then had seen Nick strolling *away* from the cottages, there was no way he could be just casually strolling before breakfast. He was living in the cottage next door.

Last night, after Nick had left, she hadn't given any thought to where he was staying. She had been too relieved that she had managed to say "no," and too busy going over every nuance of the exchange.

But the fact that Nick had stooped to the tactic with the key card and put her in a cottage next door to his underlined that he was serious about wanting her back.

She took a deep breath and let it out slowly. Just because Nick was next door didn't change anything. When he realized that she meant what she had said, he would soon switch his attention to one of the many gorgeous women she was sure would be at the resort.

After spraying herself with an ultrafeminine floral perfume, she picked up her folder of workshop notes and the quiz and strolled out of the cottage.

The restaurant was buzzing with guests enjoying breakfast and sitting on the terrace looking out over the stunning views. Relieved to see that Nick was not among the diners, Elena chose a secluded table, and ordered items that were listed on her diet maintenance plan.

Half an hour later, fortified by fresh fruit, yogurt and green tea, Elena strolled into the conference center and froze.

In a sea of femininity, Nick, dressed in black, his shoulders broad, biceps tanned, was a shady counterpart to the preponderance of white cotton, expensive jewelry and flashes of bright resort wear.

His head turned and her heart jolted as his gaze locked with hers.

Jaw firming against the instant heightened awareness and a too-vivid flashback of the previous night, Elena quickly walked to the podium and made an effort to ignore him.

Setting her folder and her laptop down on the table next to the lectern, she booted up the laptop and connected with the large state-of-the-art computerized screen. Briskly, she opened the file and checked that there were no glitches with the software. With the first slide displayed, she was good to go.

A wave of excited feminine laughter attracted her attention. A group of half a dozen of the youngest, prettiest women was clustered around Nick. *Like bees to a honeypot.*

The knowledge that, just as she'd thought, Nick was in the process of hooking up with one of the very pretty women in her seminar made her freeze in place.

She sloshed water from a jug into the tumbler beside it, barely noticing when some spilled onto the table. Setting the jug down with a sharp crack, she looked for a napkin to wipe up the spill. It shouldn't matter that Nick was making conquests, setting up his next romantic episode.

She couldn't find a napkin. Irritation morphing into annoyance, she found a notepad, which she dropped on top of the small puddle.

A sexy rumble of masculine laughter punctuated by a husky feminine voice calling to Nick jerked her head up. She was in time to see a tawny-haired woman with the kind of sultry beauty and lean, curvaceous figure that graced lingerie billboards, fling herself at Nick.

Nick's arms closed around the goddesslike creature, pulling her into a loose clinch.

In that moment, Elena registered two salient facts. Firstly, that the woman Nick was now hugging casually against his side was Nick's cousin, although only by adoption, Eva Atraeus. Secondly, that Eva *was* the kind of woman who graced underwear billboards.

Once a very successful model and now the owner of her own wedding-planning business, Eva was the feminine equivalent of a black sheep in the Atraeus family. Single and determinedly strong-willed, she had sidestepped her adoptive father's efforts to maneuver her into an advantageous marriage. Instead, she had become notorious for serially dating a number of tabloid bad boys.

Elena's stomach tightened as she watched the casual but intimate exchange. It was clear that Nick and Eva knew each other very well.

Who Nick hugged shouldn't matter. Nick Messena didn't belong to her, and he was not husband material.

He'd had his chance, *twice*.

Scrunching up the sopping wet little pad, she tossed it into a nearby trash can. Grimly, she concentrated on stacking her notes neatly on the podium and remembering her last date with Robert. Frustratingly, she couldn't recall the name of the restaurant or what she had eaten. Her one abiding memory was that she had learned just a little too much about Australian tax law.

She checked her watch. She had given herself plenty of time to set up, and consequently had a good fifteen minutes left until the official start time to mingle with her clients.

Extracting her name tag from her handbag, she fastened it on to the left shoulder of her top then walked down onto the floor of the conference room to circulate.

Nick cut her off just as she reached a table set up with coffee, green tea, a selection of wheatgrass and vegetable juices, and platters of fresh fruit. "Looks like a good turnout. Congratulations."

Elena pointedly checked her wristwatch. "We start in just a few minutes."

"I'm aware of the start time. I'm sitting in on the seminar."

Elena reached for a teacup, her careful calm already threatening to evaporate. "You can't stay."

Nick's expression was oddly neutral. "It's my resort. I'm entitled to make sure that what you're doing works for the level of service and luxury we provide."

Elena tensed at the thought of Nick sitting in on her seminar. Jaw tight, she poured herself a cup of green tea. "Constantine approved the program—"

"In the same week he handed over control to me."

With calm precision, Elena set the cup on its saucer, added a slice of lemon and tried to control an irrational spurt of panic. If Nick wanted to crash the seminar she couldn't stop him.

Last night, before she had gone to bed, she had used her priority clearance to check the Atraeus computer files for the details of the resort deal. Nick owned 51 percent. It was a reality she couldn't fight. Not only was he the majority shareholder, it would appear he was also now the current manager.

Technically, he was also her employer for the entire New Zealand group of resorts.

She held the steaming green tea in front of her like a shield. The thin, astringent scent, which she was still trying to accustom herself to, wafted to her nostrils, making her long for the richness of coffee, although she quickly quashed the thought. She was intent on cutting anything bad out of her life. Like Nick Messena, coffee was banned. "The seminar is of no possible interest to you. It's designed for women—"

"There are other men here."

Two men, both booked in by their wives. She had already checked both of them out and couldn't help noticing that they were oddly similar in appearance. Both were medium height and trim as if they ate sensibly and exercised regularly. They were also well dressed and extremely well-groomed. *Like Robert.*

With an effort of will, Elena called up Robert's image again. Right now, with Nick looming over her looking muscular and tanned, as relaxed as a big hunting cat, Robert was a touchstone she desperately needed.

Although, distressingly, she was having trouble remembering exactly what he looked like. Whenever she tried to concentrate on Robert's face, Nick Messena's strong, slightly battered features swam into view.

She kept her expression pleasant as she sipped the bitter tea and tried not to watch longingly as Nick helped himself to black coffee, adding cream and two sugars.

A clear indication that he was settling in for the duration.

She took a sip of tea and couldn't quite control her grimace. "I decided to throw the seminar open to men who were interested in improving their relationships."

"And I'm not?"

She met his gaze squarely. "You said it, not me."

"The question was rhetorical. As it happens, now that the nature of my business is changing, I'm going to have a lot more time on my hands to dedicate to…relationships."

Elena almost choked on another mouthful of tea. She glanced at Eva who had just helped herself to coffee. Unbidden, her mind made an instant wild leap. As an Atraeus employee she had heard the rumor that Eva's father, Mario, who was terminally ill, had been trying to force a match between Eva and Gabriel Messena.

The rumor had been confirmed by Gabriel's new wife, Gemma. Since Gabriel had just married, that meant Mario would be looking for another bridegroom for his headstrong daughter. Of course Nick, as the second Messena son, would be Mario's natural choice.

"No way," Nick said flatly.

Startled, Elena carefully set her tea down before she had another spill. "No way, what?"

"Eva and I are just good friends."

Elena could feel her careful control shattering, the veneer of politeness zapped by a hot burn of emotion she had no hope of controlling. "Then why is she here?"

Somewhere in the recesses of her brain she registered that she must have taken a half step toward Nick, because suddenly she was close enough that she could feel the heat from his body, smell the clean scents of soap and masculine cologne.

Nick's gaze narrowed. "You're jealous."

Elena stared at the taut line of Nick's jaw and a small scar that was almost as fascinating as the nick across the bridge of his nose. "That would be when hell freezes over."

"You don't have to worry. I'm not interested in Eva. After last night you have to know that I want you back."

A tingling thrill shot through her, cutting through the annoyance that he knew she was jealous.

He still wanted her.

A surge of delight mixed with an odd little rush of feminine power put a flush on her cheeks and jerked her chin up a little higher.

But a familiar dash of panic doused the surge of excitement. The last thing she needed to know now was that, after everything that had gone wrong, there was a chance for them after all.

He had left her twice. She should be over him, but clearly she wasn't because the dangerous, electrifying attraction was still there.

Six years. The time that had passed since they had first slept together was a dose of reality she badly needed.

Those years had been lonely and more than a little depressing because she had been unable to settle into another relationship. Like any other woman her age, she had wanted to be loved and connected to somebody special. She had wanted all the trappings of marriage, the warmth and commitment, the family home, the babies.

She hadn't come close, because in her heart of hearts she hadn't been able to move on. She had still been in love with Nick.

She went still inside, the hubbub of conversation receding as she examined the extremity of her emotions, the single-minded way she had clung to the one man who had never really wanted her.

Could she possibly still be in love with Nick?

The thought settled in with a searing, depressing finality. If so, she had loved him through her teens and for all of her adult life, eleven years and counting, with almost no encouragement at all. The chances that she could walk away from him now and get over him didn't look good.

She knew her nature. As controlled and methodical as she was in her daily life, she was also aware of a lurking streak of passionate extremity that seemed to be a part of her emotional make up. Like her aunt Katherine, she obviously had a deep need for a lasting, true love. The kind of love that was neither light nor casual, and which possessed the terrible propensity for things to go wrong.

Nick set his coffee down, untouched. "Eva's a wedding planner. This resort is one of her most requested wedding venues."

Unbidden relief made her knees feel suddenly as weak as water. "If all you want is to gauge the effectiveness of the seminar, you don't need to attend. The head therapist of the spa facility is sitting in."

Nick crossed his arms over his chest. "I'm not leaving, babe."

A secret little thrill shot down her spine at Nick's casual use of "babe," a term that carried the heady subtext that they were a couple and he was stubbornly bent on proving that fact.

A little desperately she skimmed the room and tried to restore her perspective. "I am not your *babe.*"

Ignoring the steady way he watched her, she checked her watch, set her tea back down on the table and walked back to the podium.

Once the first session started it was easier to focus. Nick, true to his word, hadn't left but was occupying a seat near the back of the room. She would have to tolerate his presence until he got tired of material he could have absolutely no interest in and left. The other two men, Harold and Irvine, obviously keen to learn, were seated in the front row.

After introducing the other speakers who were there for the day, Elena surrendered the podium to a beauty therapist who wanted to talk about the latest skin-care technology. While that was going on Elena handed out her quiz.

When she reached Nick's row, which was occupied by Eva and a couple of the more elderly women, she bypassed him without handing out a quiz sheet.

A lean hand briefly curled around her wrist, stopping

her in her tracks. "Whatever that is you're handing out, I'd like to see it."

Reluctantly she handed him the quiz. "It's not something you'd be interested in."

He studied the sheet. "As it happens, I'm pretty sure I do know what women really want."

Her temper snapped at a sudden visual of Nick with dozens of women marching through his bedroom. "Sex doesn't count."

He went still. "Maybe I'm not all about sex. You think I'll score low?"

"I think your score will be catastrophic. Most men can't get above thirty percent."

"What would you say if I believe I can score at least eighty?"

"I'd say that was impossible."

"Then you wouldn't mind a wager on that?"

She drew a swift breath. "Name it."

"You in my bed, for one more night."

She blinked at the sudden flash of heat evoked by that image.

Although, he would never get past 10 percent. She had tried the test on her male hairdresser who was used to dealing with women all day. He had aced it at 55 percent. Nick definitely didn't have a chance. "What do I get when you lose?"

"A free rein to make whatever changes you want to our spa services. And I'll leave you alone."

She met his gaze. "Done."

There was a small smattering of applause.

Embarrassed, Elena swung around to find that the entire seminar group had stopped to listen, including the beauty therapist.

The elderly lady sitting next to Nick said, "When can he do the test?"

"Now would be a good time," Elena muttered grimly.

Twenty minutes later, Elena studied Nick's test with disbelief. She had checked through on her answer sheet, a sheet that only she had access to, twice. He had scored 85 percent, and she was almost certain that he had fluffed one of the easy questions to show off.

She thought she knew Nick through and through, although she was aware that there were private glimpses of his life, like his relationship with his father, which informed her that Nick had a very private side.

Still, could she have been so wrong, and the baddest of the bad boys wasn't so bad after all?

She walked over to where Nick was standing drinking wheatgrass juice and eating sushi with an expression on his face that suggested he wasn't entirely sure that either item qualified as food. "How did you do it?"

"What was my score?"

When she told him, Nick set his wheatgrass juice down, his gaze oddly wary. "When do I get my prize?"

Elena's stomach did a somersault as the completely unacceptable sensual excitement that had proved to be her downfall, twice, leaped to life.

Her reaction made no sense, because she had no interest in a slice of the relationship cake—she wanted the whole thing. She wanted to be desperately in love with a gorgeous guy who was just as in love with her.

She wanted to wallow in the attention and the nurturing warmth of being with someone who not only wanted her but who couldn't live without her.

Nick was not that man.

At six, as part of the pamper weekend package, they were all due to go on a sunset cruise. The cruise would take up a substantial part of the evening. By the time they got back there wouldn't be much of the evening left. "Tonight."

Twelve

Nick knocked on her door at six. Feeling more than a little nervous, she checked her appearance. For the first time in her life she was wearing a bikini, a daring jungle print, concealed by a filmy green cotton tunic that fell to midthigh and was belted at her hips. The look was casual, chic and sexy.

Applying a last waft of perfume, she picked up her beach bag, slipped on matching emerald-green sandals and strolled to the door. When she opened it, Nick, still dressed in the dark trousers and polo, was lounging in the small portico talking on his cell.

His gaze skimmed the emerald-green cover-up and the length of tanned leg it revealed as he hung up. "There's been a change of plan. The motor on the resort's yacht is leaking oil, so we'll be taking mine."

Saraband.

Elena's pulse kicked up another notch at the mention

of Nick's yacht. She had seen it moored out in the bay. It was large, with elegant, racy lines.

He checked his wristwatch. "The catering staff is stocking *Saraband,* but before we cast off I need to collect a spare radio." He nodded in the direction of his Jeep, which she could glimpse, parked just beyond the trees that screened her cottage.

Long minutes later, emotion grabbed at her as Nick drove onto the manicured grounds of the Messena family home. She used to visit on occasion when her aunt was working here, but she had never actually been invited.

The house itself was a large, Victorian old lady with a colonnaded entrance and wraparound verandas top and bottom, giving it a grand, colonial air.

Ultrasensitive to Nick's presence and the knowledge that she had agreed to sleep with him again, *tonight,* Elena climbed out of the Jeep before Nick could get around to help her.

Nick strolled up the steps with her and held the front door.

Removing her sunglasses, Elena stepped into the shady hall.

Nick gestured at a large, airy sitting room with comfortable cream couches floating on a gleaming hardwood floor. French doors led onto a patio, a sweep of green lawn added to the feeling of tranquillity. "Make yourself at home—I won't be long. Eva's staying here for the duration of the retreat but, other than her, the house is empty."

Elena stiffened at the mention of Eva's name.

Firming her chin, she banished the too-familiar insecurities. She had committed to spend the night with Nick. She would not lose her nerve or allow herself to imagine that she wasn't attractive enough for him. It wasn't as if they had never spent a night together. They had. Twice.

Taking a steadying breath, she checked out the sun-washed patio with its pretty planters overflowing with gardenias and star jasmine, then stepped back inside, blinking as her vision adjusted to the shady dimness.

She had already reasoned out her approach. The whole idea of challenging Nick to the quiz had been a mistake. She would never in her wildest dreams have imagined that he could score so highly.

Now that he had, it was up to her to create a positive for herself out of the experience. It was an ideal opportunity to demystify the exciting passion that she now realized had blocked her from experiencing the true love she needed.

Both other times their lovemaking had been spontaneous and a little wild. This time she was determined that out-of-control passion would not be a factor. If Nick wanted to get her into bed, he would have to woo her, something she was convinced—despite his meteoric test score—that he would fail at, miserably.

Once he was exposed as superficial, unfeeling, basically dysfunctional and terrible husband material, she should be able to forget him and move on.

In theory....

She strolled to a sideboard covered with family photographs. Idly she studied an old-fashioned, touched-up wedding photo of Stefano and Luisa, and a variety of baby and family photos. She halted beside a large framed color photo of a plump, bespectacled boy in a wheelchair. It was clearly one of the Messena children, or perhaps a cousin, although she couldn't ever remember anyone mentioning that there was a disabled member of the family.

She studied the young teenager's nose, which had been broken at some point, perhaps in the accident that had injured him, and froze, drawn by an inescapable sense of familiarity. A split second later she was aware that Nick was in the room. When she turned, she logged that he had changed into faded, glove-soft denims and a white, V-necked T-shirt that hugged his shoulders and chest. A duffel bag was slung over one shoulder and he was carrying the spare radio he needed.

She looked at the framed photo of the boy in the wheelchair then transferred her gaze to Nick's nose.

The wariness of his expression killed any uncertainty she might have had stone dead. "That's you."

"At age sixteen."

She could feel the firm emotional ground she had been occupying shift, throwing her subtly off balance. She could remember her aunt mentioning that Nick had had an accident, she had just never imagined it had been that bad.

Just when she thought she had Nick in focus, something changed and she had to reevaluate. The last thing she wanted to learn now was that Nick had a past hurt, that he had been vulnerable, that maybe there were depths she had missed. "What happened?"

"A rugby accident." He shrugged. "It's old history now. I was playing in a trial game for a place at Auckland Boy's Grammar and their rugby academy. I got hit with a bad tackle and broke my back."

Nodding his head at the door, he indicated that they needed to leave, but Elena wasn't finished.

"How long were you overweight?"

He held the door for her, his expression now distinctly impatient. "About a year. Until I started to walk again."

"Long enough not to like how it felt."

"I guess you could say that."

Her mind racing, Elena followed him outside and

neatly avoided his offer of assistance as she climbed into the Jeep's front passenger seat.

Her fingers fumbling as she fastened the seat belt, she tried to move briskly past this setback. She thought she'd had Nick all figured out, that he was callous and shallow, but it was worse than that.

He had a nice streak, a compassionate, protective instinct that she could relate to with every cell of her body. When she was a kid, she had automatically protected every other overweight kid. She hadn't been able to help it; she had felt their vulnerability when they got picked on.

Nick shared that trait in common with her because he had been in that same depressing place, *and* with the glasses. "Is that why you stepped in as my blind date, then slept with me?"

Nick frowned. "The reason I stepped in on your blind date is that I couldn't stand the thought of Smale getting his hands on you. And it wasn't just because I wanted to protect you," he said grimly. "Babe, believe it. I wanted you for myself."

Nick maneuvered the *Saraband* into a sheltered crescent bay on Honeymoon Island, a small jewel of an island about three miles offshore from the resort.

He started lowering the anchor. While he waited for the chain to stop feeding out, he looked over the bow.

Elena had spent the first part of the trip circulating with the clients, but for the past fifteen minutes she had been a solitary figure sitting on the bow, staring out to sea.

Nick jammed his finger on the button, stopping the anchor chain from feeding out. Impatience ate at his normally rock-solid composure while he waited for the yacht to swing around in the breeze. He took a further minute to check line-of-sight bearings to ensure that the anchor had locked securely on to the seabed and that they weren't drifting. By the time he walked out onto the deck, the first boat, with Elena aboard, was already heading for the bay.

His gaze was remote as he slipped a pair of dark glasses onto the bridge of his nose. No doubt about it, she was avoiding him.

Not that he would let her do that for long.

She needed some space. He might not be the sensitive, New Age guy she thought she wanted. Over the next few hours he intended to prove to her that he was the man she needed.

Two hours later, annoyed with the champagne and the canapés, and the fact that Elena seemed intent on having long, heartfelt conversations with the two men attending the seminar, Harold and Irvine, Nick decided to take action.

He didn't dislike Harold, though something about Irvine set him on edge. Though both were married, he wasn't about to underestimate either of them. Harold, at least, was a carbon copy of the guy Elena was lining up to be her future husband.

By the time he had extracted himself from a conversation with a pretty blonde, the kind of friendly, confident woman he was normally attracted to, Elena had disappeared.

Annoyed, he skimmed the beach and the array of bathers lying beneath colorful resort beach umbrellas. There was no flash of the green tunic Elena had been wearing. After having a quick word with Harold, who was now immersed in a book, he followed a lone set of footprints.

Rounding a corner, he found a small private beach

overhung with pohutukawa trees in blossom, their deep red flowers a rich accent to gray-green leaves and honey-colored sand. Beneath the tree, in a pool of dappled shade, lay Elena's beach bag and the green tunic.

He looked out to sea and saw her swimming with slow, leisurely grace. His jaw tightened when he saw a second swimmer closing in on Elena. Irvine.

Out of habit, suspicious of the motives of men who wanted to come on a course designed for women, he had done some checking and received the information just minutes before. Harold had proved to be exactly as he appeared, a businessman intent on trying to please a dominant wife. Irvine, however, had a background that was distinctly unpleasant.

Nick shrugged out of his T-shirt and peeled off his jeans, revealing the swimming trunks he was wearing beneath. Jogging to the water, he waded to the break line. A few quick strokes through choppy waves and he was gliding through deep water.

A piercing shriek shoved raw adrenaline through his veins. Irvine was treading water beside Elena, holding his nose. Relief eased some of his tension as he logged the fact that it was Irvine, not Elena, who had shrieked. The source of the outraged cry was clear in the bloody nose Irvine was nursing.

An odd mixture of pride and satisfaction coursed through Nick as he saw Elena slicing through the waves toward him, her strokes workmanlike and efficient. Irvine had clearly thought he had caught Elena vulnerable and alone—no doubt his favorite modus operandi—and she had quickly dispelled that idea with a solid punch to the nose.

Irvine finally noticed Nick, and went white as a sheet.

Nick didn't need to utter a threat—the long steady look was message enough. He would deal with Irvine later.

Elena splashed to a halt beside him. "Did you see what Irvine did?"

Nick watched Irvine's progress as he gave them a wide berth and dog-paddled haltingly in the direction of the crowded beach. "I was too busy trying to get to you in time."

She treaded water. "You knew about Irvine?"

Nick dragged his gaze from the tantalizing view through the water of a sexy jungle-print bikini and the curves it revealed. "I ran a security check on him this morning. I received the results a few minutes ago."

Nick's hands closed around Elena's arms as the swell pushed her in close against him. "He has a police record and no wife. Did he touch you?"

The question was rough and flat, but the thought that Irvine had laid hands on Elena sent a cold fire shooting through his veins.

"He didn't touch me—he didn't get the chance. It was more what he said."

"Let me guess, he wanted 'sexual therapy' to help him with his problems?"

Another wave drove Elena closer still, so that their legs tangled and their bodies bumped. Automatically, she grasped his shoulders. "That's what's stated on his police record?"

"He targets therapists. Lately he's been doing the rounds of the health spas. Although this will be his last attempt."

"You're going to get him." Her gaze was intense and laced with the kind of admiration that made his heart swell in his chest. Finally, he was doing something right. He stared, mesmerized at her golden, flowerlike irises and wondered how she could ever have reached the conclusion that she had to change those. "I'll sic my lawyers onto him as soon as we get in."

Leaning forward, she touched her mouth to his. "Thank you."

The kiss deepened. He fitted her close against him, acutely aware of the smoothness of her skin against his, the tiny span of her waist and the delicacy of her curves.

The moment when he had realized that Irvine had swum after her replayed itself.

Unconsciously, his hold on Elena tightened. He had let her out of his sight, too busy brooding over the easy way she had shut him out, and Irvine had taken his chance. That wouldn't happen again. From now on, he would make certain that Elena was protected at all times.

Messena women routinely required protection because the amount of wealth his family possessed made them a target. Elena hadn't agreed to a relationship with him— *yet*—but even so, she would accept his protection. There was a small clause in all Atraeus and Messena employment contracts he could exploit if he needed to.

She wouldn't like it, but as far as he was concerned, until Irvine was put behind bars, Elena wouldn't move more than a few paces without either him or a bodyguard protecting her.

When she pulled back and released her hold, Nick had to forcibly restrain himself from reaching for her again. Instead, when she indicated that she wanted to head for shore, he contented himself with swimming with slow, leisurely strokes so she could easily keep pace.

As he waded from the water, satisfaction eased some of his tension when he saw Irvine still struggling in the surf, holding his nose.

When Elena stepped out of the water and Nick got his

first real look at the bikini, he felt as though he'd been punched in the stomach. With her hair a satiny cap, her skin sleek with water, she was both exotic and stunning. The bikini revealed long, elegant legs and the kind of slim, curvaceous figure that made his mouth water, the bright jungle print giving Elena's skin a tawny glow.

He had always registered that she was pretty and attractive, but now she took his breath.

As Elena reached for the towel she had tossed down on the sand, a scuffling sound attracted Nick's attention. Harold, the carbon copy of the sainted Robert, was walking over the rocks, his gaze firmly fixed on Elena.

"That's it," he muttered. "No more men on your weekend seminars."

Elena wrapped the towel around herself and knotted it, successfully concealing almost every part of the bikini but the halter tie around her neck. Her first outing in the skimpy swimming costume had been a disaster. After the unhealthy way Irvine had looked at her, his eyes practically glowing, she was over revealing her new body. "Harold's harmless."

The complete opposite of Nick, who, with his gaze narrowed and glittering as he regarded Harold's halting progress, looked both tough and formidable. "Like Irvine?"

A shudder went through her. "Point made."

She noted that Harold's gaze was riveted on her chest. Her stomach plunged. She suddenly wished she hadn't spent so much time talking to Harold, who seemed to have misconstrued her intentions. "Do you think—?"

Nick said something short and sharp beneath his breath. "You should know by now that if you spend time with a guy, chances are he's going to think you're interested in him."

Elena recoiled from the concept of Harold falling in clinging lust with her. Reinventing herself and wearing the alluring clothes she had always longed to wear had an unexpected dark side. "That hasn't been my experience."

Nick's gaze sliced back to hers. "You've dated. I checked."

"You *pried* into my personal life?"

"You work for the Atraeus Group. We now share a database in common."

"You accessed my personal file." A file that did contain a list of the men she had dated. Working as a PA to both Lucas then Zane Atraeus, she was privy to confidential information and anyone she dated was also scrutinized.

Elena's intense irritation that Nick was poking his nose into her private affairs was almost instantly replaced by a spiraling sense of delight that he was worried enough to do so.

Her attention was momentarily diverted as Harold unfastened his shirt and tossed it on the sand, revealing an unexpectedly tanned, toned torso. "I don't think I'll include men in the pamper program again."

Nick's head swung in Harold's direction, and he muttered a soft oath. "Include men, babe, and you can bank on it that I'll be there."

The blunt possessiveness of his attitude, combined with the way he had come after her to protect her from Irvine, filled Elena with the kind of wild, improbable hope she knew she should squash. Hope messed with her focus. She needed to approach this night together exactly as Nick would—as a pleasurable interlude from which she could walk away unscathed.

Nick's gaze dropped to her mouth. "If you want to get rid of Harold, you should kiss me again."

A shaft of heat at the prospect of another passionate, off-the-register kiss seared through her. "It's not exactly professional."

"The hell with professional."

As Nick's hands settled at her waist, the clinical list of things she would absolutely not allow was swamped by another wave of pure desire. Before she could stop herself, mouth dry, heart pounding a wild tattoo, she stepped close and slid her palms over the muscled swell of his shoulders.

Without the cool water that had swirled around them out at sea, Nick's skin was hot to the touch. Taking a deep breath, she went up on her toes and fitted herself more closely against him.

The instant her mouth touched his, she forgot about Irvine and Harold, and she forgot about the strategy she'd decided upon. Streamers of heat seemed to shimmer out from each point of contact as Nick gathered her closer still, his arms a solid bar in the small of her back.

A small thrill went through her as her feet left the ground and she found it necessary to wind her arms around Nick's neck and hang on. The situation was absolutely contrary to her plan to control her emotions and keep her heart intact, to inform Nick that she was not the easy, forgettable conquest she'd been in the past.

Dimly, she registered that the towel had peeled away and that she was sealed against Nick from thigh to mouth. Long, dizzying minutes later, a rhythmic, vibrating sound broke the dazed grip of passion.

Elena identified the sound as the ringtone of a cell, emanating from Nick's jeans, which were tossed on the sand beside her beach bag.

With a searing glance, Nick released his hold on her.

Stumbling a little in the sand and again conscious of the brevity of the bikini, Elena noticed that Harold had disappeared. She snatched up her tunic.

By the time she'd pulled the filmy tunic over her head and smoothed it down over her hips, Nick had walked several paces away. His back was turned for privacy and he seemed totally immersed in his call.

She caught the phrases "construction crew" and "form work," which meant the call was work related.

Despite the heat that radiated from the sand and seemed to float on the air, Elena felt abruptly chilled at the swiftness with which Nick had switched from passion to work.

Retrieving her towel, she tried not to focus on the pang of hurt, or a bone-deep, all-too-familiar sense of inevitability.

Of course work would come first with Nick. Hadn't it always? It wasn't as if she had ever proved to be a fascinating, irresistible lover to him.

What they had shared was passionate, and to her, beautiful and unique, but it was as if she had never truly connected with Nick. She was certain Nick had the capacity to return love, she just didn't believe it would be with her on the receiving end.

She rummaged in her green tote, found her sunglasses and jammed them onto the bridge of her nose. In the process, her fingers brushed against a book of lovemaking techniques she had bought online. Her cheeks warmed at the research she'd embarked upon because she felt so hopelessly out of her depth in that area. It was part of her general makeover; although the whole idea of planning lovemaking became irrelevant around Nick. It just happened.

She was still reeling from the last kiss and the notion that he wanted her as much as she wanted him.

As if he couldn't get enough of her.

Nick pulled on his jeans and T-shirt and slipped the phone into his pocket. "Time to go."

The searing reality of what would happen when they got back to the resort stopped the breath in her throat. "We've only been here an hour."

"An hour too long, as far as I'm concerned." Snagging her towel and beach bag, Nick held out his hand to her.

Elena's breath caught in her throat at the sudden softness in his gaze, an out-of-the-blue sense of connection that caught her off guard. It was the kind of warming intimacy she had dreamed about and wanted. As if they were friends as well as lovers. Something caught in her throat, her heart, abruptly turning her plans upside down. A conviction that there really was something special between them, something that refused to fade away and die, despite the attempts both of them had made to starve it out of existence.

Nick might not recognize what it was, yet, but she did. It was love.

And not just any love. If she wasn't mistaken, this was the bona fide, once-in-a-lifetime love she had dreamed about. The dangerous kind of love that broke hearts and changed lives, and which she had longed for ever since that one night with Nick six years ago.

From one heartbeat to the next the conflict of making love with Nick when she was supposed to be keeping him at arm's length zapped out of existence to be replaced with a new, clear-cut priority.

Making love with Nick was no longer an untenable risk or an exercise in control; it was imperative.

As crazy as it seemed with everything that had gone

wrong, they were at a crucial tipping point in their relationship. Now was not the time to shrink back and make conservative choices; passion was called for.

By some fateful chance, Nick had taken her quiz and given her an insight into aspects of his personality she would not have believed were there. The kind of warmth and consideration that would make him perfect husband material.

On the heels of that, she had unraveled a piece of his past in the disabled, overweight boy with glasses he had once been.

She had agreed to spend the night in his bed.

Her heart pounded at the thought of the passionate hours that lay ahead, their third night together.

Nick had gone out on a limb to get her back, even if he couldn't quite express his intentions, yet. She was now convinced that the risk she had taken twice before, and which each time had failed, was now viable.

It was up to her to help Nick feel emotionally secure enough to make the final step into an actual relationship. To do what, in her heart of hearts, she had wanted him to for years: to finally fall in love with her.

Thirteen

Nick marshaled the guests back onto the yacht with the promise of free champagne, cocktails and dessert when they reached the resort. The regular manager would probably have a heart attack when he saw the damage to his bottom line on this particular venture, but the way Nick saw it, his night with Elena took precedence.

He had engineered a window of opportunity. He wasn't going to let that time be eroded because clients wanted more time on the beach.

When Irvine stepped aboard, Nick intercepted him and suggested they both go below.

Irvine's expression turned belligerent. "You can't give me orders. I'm a paying guest."

Nick stepped a little closer to Irvine, deliberately crowding him and at the same time blocking him, and their very private conversation, from the rest of the guests. "You also tried to molest Ms. Lyon."

His gaze turned steely. "You can't prove that."

"Maybe not, but we can have some fun trying."

Irvine tried to peer over his shoulder. "Now I'm scared. Elena wouldn't lay charges."

Aware that Elena was conducting a conversation with some of the guests on the bow, Nick moved to block Irvine's view. "Let me see. This would be the same Elena Lyon who has a double degree that she shelved in favor of being Lucas Atraeus's personal assistant for five years."

Irvine's Adam's apple bobbed. "*The* Lucas Atraeus—?"

"Who engineered a number of mining company and resort takeovers and tipped over a major construction company that tried to use substandard steel on one of his developments." Nick crossed his arms over his chest. "Elena might look little and cute, but she orchestrated Lucas's schedule, monitored his calls, including the death threats, and deployed security when required."

Irvine paled. "I don't get it. If she's that high-powered, what's she doing in Dolphin Bay?"

"Spending time with me." Nick jerked his chin in the direction of the two inflatable boats that, on his instructions, hadn't yet been tied at the stern and were still bobbing against the side of the yacht. "I'll make things even simpler for you. If you don't go below, you can stay on the island until I come back to get you. After that, it's a one way trip to the Dolphin Bay Police Station."

After a taut moment, Irvine visibly deflated. With a shrug, he started down the stairs.

Nick followed him and indicated a seat in the dining area, positioned so Nick could keep an eye on him while he was at the wheel.

Expression set, Irvine sat. "Who could know that there would be a police station in a hick town like this?"

"Just one guy—that's all Dolphin Bay needs. And as

luck would have it, he happens to be a relative." A distant uncle, on his mother's side.

Irvine seemed to shrink into himself even further at that last piece of information. Satisfied that he was contained for the moment, Nick went topside and skimmed the deck, looking for Harold. Relief filled him as he noted that Harold had evidently given up on Elena and now seemed to be directing all of his charm toward Eva.

Eva caught his gaze for a split second and winked.

Grim humor lightened Nick's mood as he logged exactly what she was doing—running interference. Somehow, with the scary talent Eva had for figuring out exactly what was going on in men's heads, she had summed up the situation and taken charge of Harold before Nick chucked him over the side.

Minutes later, after starting the yacht's motor, then weighing anchor, Nick took the wheel. A faint, enticingly feminine floral scent informed him that Elena was close. Turning his head, he met her frowning gaze.

"What did you do with Irvine?"

"Don't worry, I didn't hit him. He's in containment." He indicated the glass panel that gave a view into the dining room below.

Satisfaction eased the tension on Elena's face. "Good, I don't want him causing trouble for any of my clients. Bad for business."

"That's my girl."

Her gaze locked with his, the absence of levity informing him that she hadn't liked the situation with Harold or Irvine one little bit. Her reaction was a stark reminder that no matter how strong or efficient Elena seemed, when it came to men she was in definite need of protection.

He had to resist the urge to pull her close and tuck

her against his side. There was no need for the primitive methods he had employed on the beach. Irvine was controlled and he had made arrangements to have him removed from the resort as soon as they reached Dolphin Bay.

As much as he would like to lay a formal complaint againt Irvine, he was aware there wasn't anything concrete that Irvine could be charged with since all he had done was make an advance, which Elena had rebuffed. Besides, police procedure took time. Elena was exclusively his for just a few hours. He wasn't going to waste that time trying to get Irvine locked up.

His jaw tightened at the thought that one more night might be all they'd have. The desire for more than a sexual liaison settled in more powerfully. The thought process was new, but he was adjusting.

Elena crossed her arms over her chest as the yacht picked up speed, hugging the thin fabric of her tunic against her skin. She sent a worried glance in Eva's direction. "Will Eva be okay?"

Satisfaction at Elena's total rejection of Harold, with his smooth good looks, eased some of Nick's tension. He spared another glance for Eva and Harold, and noted the change in Harold's body language. The expansive confidence was gone and his shoulders had slumped. He no longer seemed to be enjoying the conversation. "Don't worry about Eva. She can spot 'married' from a mile off."

"A consequence of being in the wedding business, I suppose."

Nick lifted a hand at the deckhand who had secured the inflatables. "Eva came from a broken home before Mario adopted her. She's never placed much trust in relationships."

Elena slipped sunglasses onto the bridge of her nose

and gripped a railing as the yacht picked up speed. "Sounds like a family trait."

Aware that Elena was maneuvering the conversation into personal territory he usually avoided, Nick made an attempt to relax. "Maybe."

A heavy silence formed, the kind of waiting silence he had gotten all too used to with his own family.

Elena sent him a frustrated look. "Trying to get information out of you is like talking to a sphinx."

"Seems to me I've heard that phrase somewhere before."

"Let me guess... Your sisters." She tucked errant strands of hair behind one ear, revealing the three tiny blue-green jewels that sparkled like droplets of light in her lobe.

"And the head inquisitor—my mom." He steered around a curving lacework of rocks and reefs that partially enclosed the bay. "What, exactly, do you want to know?"

She met his gaze squarely. "What you like to eat for breakfast, because we've never actually had breakfast together. Why you went into construction when the family business is banking, and..." She hesitated, her chin coming up. "What's your idea of a romantic date?"

"I like coffee and toast for breakfast, I went into construction because while I was disabled Dad taught me how to design and build a boat, and my favorite date is... anything to do with a yacht. Don't you want to ask me about my relationship dysfunction?"

"I intended to skirt around that question, but now that you've brought it up, why haven't you ever been in a long-term relationship?"

In the instant she asked the question, the answer was crystal clear to Nick. Because he had never quite been able to forget what it had felt like making love with Elena. Or that she had waited until she was twenty-two to make love, and then she had chosen *him*.

His jaw clamped against the uncharacteristic urge to spill that very private, intimate revelation. "I've got a busy schedule."

"Not too busy to date, at last count, twenty-three girls in the last two years. That's not quite one a month."

Fierce satisfaction filled him at the clear evidence that Elena was jealous. There could be no other reason for the meticulous investigation of his dating past. "That many?"

Her gaze was fiery and accusing. "I thought it would be more."

He increased speed as the water changed color from murky green to indigo, signaling deep water and a cold ocean current. Against all the odds, he was suddenly enjoying the exchange. "You should stop reading the gossip columnists. Some of those so-called dates were business acquaintances or friends."

"Huh."

He suppressed a grin and the urge to pull Elena close, despite her prickly mood. Instead, he made an adjustment to the wheel. With no more rocks or reefs to navigate, and the bow pointed in the direction of the resort's small marina, he could relax more. He found there was something oddly sweet about just being with Elena.

Glancing down into the dining room below, he noted that Irvine was still sitting exactly where Nick had placed him, although his face was now an interesting shade of green.

The conversation he'd had with Irvine replayed. It occurred to Nick that the reason he hadn't been able to walk away from Elena this time was exactly the same reason Irvine needed to back up a step.

Elena had changed over the years, even since their meeting in Cutler's office in Auckland, morphing from the quiet, introverted girl who used to watch him from the beach into a fiery, exciting butterfly with a will of steel.

His stomach tightened. She was gorgeous and fascinating. He could understand why Harold and Irvine had been dazzled, why she could keep a successful businessman like Robert Corrado on ice while she pursued her new career.

If there had ever truly been anything soft or yielding about Elena, like her old image, it was long gone.

Elena turned her head away from him, into the wind, the movement presenting him with the pure line of her profile and emphasizing her independence. After years of single life, it occurred to Nick that she was happy with her own company. Abruptly annoyed by that streak of independence, a strength that informed Nick that, as attracted as Elena was to him she didn't need him in her life, he finally gave in to the urge to pull her close.

She softened almost instantly, fitting easily into his side. Despite that, he was uneasily aware that something important was missing between them. That something was trust.

He needed to come clean about the quiz and release her from the night she had forfeited.

But that was a risk he wasn't prepared to take. If he released Elena before he'd had a chance to bind her to him in the hours ahead, he wasn't certain he would be able to convince her that she should refocus her attention.

Away from Robert Corrado and onto *him*.

Elena, still uneasily aware of both Harold and Irvine, was more than happy to leave the yacht with her clients when they docked at the small jetty.

With satisfaction, she noted both Irvine and Harold being ushered by Nick into a resort vehicle that appeared to also contain their luggage. The driver of the vehicle was one of the gardeners she'd noticed, a burly man who looked as though he had once been a boxer.

Nick strolled alongside her as she entered the resort restaurant. Waiters were already circulating with trays of champagne and canapés. Lifting two flutes from a tray, he pressed one into her hand then began ushering her toward the door.

"We're leaving now?" she asked.

"It is almost eight."

A small thrill of excitement shot through Elena. She had thought they might have dinner and maybe dance on the terrace, but Nick's hurry to get her to himself was somehow more alluring than a slow, measured seduction.

And technically their bargain terminated at midnight. Her stomach clenched at the thought of four hours alone with Nick. "Uh—what about dinner?"

He stopped, his hand on the doorknob. "We can get room service. Although, if you'd prefer to stay here for dinner, we can do that."

His expression was oddly neutral, his voice clipped. If she didn't know Nick better, she would think that eating here and losing time alone together didn't really matter, but she knew the opposite to be true, and in a flash she got him.

Nick was utterly male. Naturally, he didn't like emotion, and in the world he moved, showing any form of emotion would be deemed a weakness. She knew that much from working with both Lucas and Zane Atraeus. The only time they truly relaxed was when they were with their families.

Carla and Lilah had made comments that when their

men felt the most, they closed up even more. Getting actual words out of them was like squeezing blood out of the proverbial stone.

Carla and Lilah had been describing Lucas and Zane, but the description also fit Nick.

Her heart pounded at a breakthrough that put a different slant on some of the starkest moments in her relationship with Nick and made sense of his extreme reaction to his father's death. Nick walked away, not because he didn't care, but because he cared too much. "I don't need to eat."

"I was hoping you would say that."

She took a hurried gulp of the fizzy champagne so it wouldn't spill as they walked. The walkway was smooth enough, but with the shadowy shapes of palms and thick tropical plantings plunging parts of it into deep shadow it would be easy to stumble. She took another sip and noticed the moon was up. "I'm for room service."

His quick grin made her stomach flip. She hadn't thought the night would be fun. She'd thought it would be too fraught with the tensions that seemed to be a natural part of their relationship.

The fact that she was applying the term "relationship" to herself and Nick sent a small, effervescent thrill shimmering all the way to her toes. Finally, after years of being stalled, and just when she had thought all was lost, they were finally in an actual relationship. She felt like hugging him, she felt like dancing—

"Okay, what's going on?"

Nick was eyeing her with caution, which made her feel even more giddily happy, because it was clear he had noted what she was feeling. He was *reading* her mood.

There was only one reason for that to happen. He was concerned about her happiness; he was beginning to *care*.

It wasn't love, yet, but they were definitely getting closer. "I'm…" She suppressed the dangerous, undisciplined urge to blurt out that she was head over heels in love with him and had been for years. "I'm happy."

His gaze slid to the half-empty flute.

Elena took a deep breath and tried to drag her gaze from the fascinating pulse beating on the side of his jaw. "It's not the champagne." She examined the pale liquid with its pretty bubbles and without regret tossed what was left into the depths of a leafy green shrub. "I don't need champagne to spend the night with you."

To make gorgeous, tender, maybe even adventurous love with the man she loved.

For a split second the night seemed to go still, the tension thick enough to cut. "You don't have to sleep with me if you don't want. The quiz was a spur-of-the-moment thing. I shouldn't have—"

"We have a bargain. You *can't* back out."

Startlement registered in his expression. Relief flooded Elena. She had been desperately afraid he was going to release her from their deal. By her estimation the next few hours together were crucial. If they didn't make love and dissolve the last frustrating, invisible barriers between them, they might never have another chance.

In response, Nick reeled her in close with his free hand, fitting her tightly enough against him that she could feel his masculine arousal. "Does this feel like I'm backing out?"

The breath hitched in her throat at the graphic knowledge that Nick very definitely wanted her. "No."

"Good, because I'm not."

He took the flute from her and set it down with his own on the arm of a nearby wooden bench. Taking her hand, he drew her down the short path to his cottage.

The warm light from his porch washed over taut cheekbones and the solid line of his jaw as, without releasing her hand, he unlocked the door and pushed it wide.

Instead of standing to one side to allow her to precede him, Nick stepped toward her. At first, Elena thought he wanted to kiss her, then the world spun dizzily as he swung her into his arms.

Startled, Elena clutched at Nick's shoulders as he stepped into the lit hall and kicked the door closed behind him. Seconds later he set her on her feet in the middle of a large room lit by the flicker of candles and smelling of flowers. Heart still pounding, and pleasure humming through her at a gesture that was traditionally shared by a bride and groom, Elena inhaled the perfume of lavish bunches of white roses.

Nick took his cell out of his pocket and placed it on a workstation in a small alcove that also contained a laptop and a file. The small action made her intensely aware that, for the first time ever, she was in Nick's personal quarters—not his home, because the resort cottage was only a temporary accommodation, but in his private space.

Elena strolled to one of the vases of flowers.

"Do you like them?"

Throat tight with emotion, Elena touched a delicate petal with one fingertip. She was trying to be sensible and pragmatic, trying not to get her hopes too high, but she couldn't *not* feel wonder and pleasure at the trouble Nick had gone to.

Even though the room, with its candles and flowers, had most probably been staged by one of the resort professionals, it was still quite possibly the most romantic gesture any man had ever made. More wonderful than the traditional red roses Robert had sent to her. Even though she had been thrilled to receive the bouquet, thrilled at the fact that for the first time in her life she was being wooed, Robert's dozen red roses hadn't made her heart squeeze tight.

Blinking back the moisture that seemed to be filling her eyes, she straightened. "I love white roses. How did you know?"

"I got my PA to research what flowers you liked." Nick picked up a remote from a low teak coffee table and pressed a button. A tango filled the air, sending an instant thrill down her spine and spinning her back to the steamy tango they had danced at Gemma's wedding.

Determinedly, she dismissed the small core of disappointment that had formed at the systematic, logical way Nick had selected the flowers for their night together. Using a PA was a very corporate solution. She should know; she had done similar personal tasks herself for her Atraeus bosses.

Nick may not have personally known what flowers she liked, he may not have staged the room, but he had arranged it for her pleasure.

She forced herself to move on from the flowers and examined the rest of the interior. Furnished with dark leather couches, low tables and exotic teak armoires, the stark masculinity was relieved by a pile of yachting books on a side table and an envelope of what looked like family snapshots.

The family photos, some of which had slid out of the envelope, riveted her attention because they proved that Nick loved his family, that at a bedrock level, relationships were vitally important to him.

She sensed Nick's approach a moment before he turned her around and drew her into his arms. The tango wound its sinuous way through the candlelit room as she allowed him to pull her closer still and the night seemed to take on an aching throb. Filled with an utter sense of rightness, Elena wound her arms around Nick's neck and went up on her toes to touch her mouth to his.

Long, drugging seconds later, Nick lifted his head. "That's the first time you've actually kissed me properly."

"I've changed." Elena concentrated on keeping her expression serene. As tempted as she was to let Nick take control, to simply abandon herself to sensation, she couldn't afford to get lost in a whirlwind of passion as she had done on the last two occasions. To maximize her chances of success with him, she needed to keep her head and control her responses.

Threading her fingers through Nick's hair, she pulled his mouth back to hers.

Conditions were not ideal for the love scene she had thought would take place. For one thing, she hadn't had time to slip into the sexy lingerie, or the jersey silk dress she had intended to wear. She hadn't had the chance to shower or use the expensive body lotion she had bought, which would have been a more pleasant alternative to the residue of sea salt on her skin.

She couldn't allow any of that to matter. Luckily, she had remembered to pack the book of lovemaking techniques in her beach bag, intending to read it on the beach, so at least she could attempt to be a little more sophisticated than she'd been on previous occasions.

As if in response to the sensuality sizzling in the air, the tango music grew smokier.

Feeling a little nervy, Elena dragged at the buttons of Nick's shirt. As she unfastened the last button, she watched, mouth dry as Nick shrugged out of it, letting the limp cotton drop to the floor.

With his shirt off, his shoulders muscular and gleaming in the glow of candlelight, his chest broad and abs washboard tight, Nick was beautiful in a completely masculine way. The dark hair sprinkled across his chest and arrowed to the waistband of his pants, adding an earthy edge that made her pulse race. He pulled her close for another kiss, this one deeper, longer than the last.

Once again, determined to take the initiative, Elena found the waistband of Nick's pants and tugged, pulling Nick with her as she walked backward in the direction of the bedrooms.

If this cottage was the same as hers, and so far it looked identical, the master bedroom would be a short walk down the hall and to the left, with a set of doors opening out onto the terrace.

She managed to maneuver a step to the right so she could grab the strap of her beach bag on the way.

Nick lifted his head, his brows jerking together when he noticed the bag, but by then they were in the hall and the ultimate destination of the bedroom was clear.

The plan stalled for a few seconds when Nick planted one hand on the doorjamb, preventing further progress. He cupped her jaw, sliding the pad of his thumb over her bottom lip in a caress that made her head spin. "Maybe we should slow this down—"

"You mean wait?" A little breathlessly, Elena tugged at the annoyingly difficult fastening of his jeans. By now, Nick should have been naked.

Fourteen

Nick's palm curled around to cup her nape. "Are you sure this is what you want? I had planned something a little more—"

She found the zipper and dragged it down.

Nick made an odd groaning sound. "Uh, never mind…" With a deft movement, he undid what looked like a double fastening and peeled out of the jeans.

Elena's mouth went dry. With Nick wearing nothing more than the swimming trunks he'd had on beneath his jeans while she was still fully dressed, the sexual initiative should have been hers, a clear message to him that she was no longer a novice at this. But with the golden wash of light from the sitting room flaring over taut, bronzed muscles and adding a heated gleam to his gaze, there was no hint that Nick had registered the dominating tactic. He looked utterly, spectacularly at home in his own skin.

Seconds later, in a further reversal, Elena found herself propelled gently backward into the bedroom. She remembered to hang on to the strap of the bag, which had slipped off her shoulder and hooked around her wrist. Having to concentrate on keeping the bag and the book with her was an unexpected boon, because the sensual control she'd worked so hard to establish was rapidly dissolving into an array of delicious sensations that made it very hard to think.

Nick's fingers brushed her nape. Heat surged through her as she felt the neckline of her tunic loosen. Cool air flowed against her skin as the tunic slipped to her waist, trapping her arms.

Nick took advantage of her trapped arms to bend and brush his lips over one shoulder. The featherlight kiss sent another throb of sensual heat through her, before she dropped her bag and finally managed to wriggle her arms free.

A split second later the entire tunic floated to the floor, informing her that while she had been concentrating on the logistics of moving Nick into the bedroom, his fingers had been busy undoing the entire line of buttons that ran down her back.

A wave of melting heat zinged through her as Nick's hands cupped her breasts through the thin Lycra of her bikini. Dipping his head, he took one breast into his mouth, and for long, shimmering moments she lost focus as the aching throb low in her belly gathered and tightened.

Dimly, she noted that this part of the seduction was not going to plan. She had hoped to keep all of her clothes on until the last moment. Somehow things had deteriorated to the point that she was in danger of being naked first and once more irresistibly propelled into a whirlpool of passion.

Nick transferred his attention to her mouth. Without thinking, her arms coiled around his neck as she arched into the kiss and fitted herself more closely against him. With a slick movement, he picked her up and deposited her on the bed, following her down and sprawling beside her.

She felt a tug at her hips, the coolness of air as her bikini bottoms were stripped down her legs. Her brain snapped back into gear when she realized that for a few seconds she had allowed herself to drift in a pleasurable daze and now was completely naked.

Bracing her palms on Nick's chest, she pushed.

He frowned. "You want to be on top?"

She drew a deep breath. "Yes." The position was the most basic in the book, but it had the advantage of being easy to remember.

Obligingly, he subsided onto his back. Taking a deep breath, Elena began the business of peeling the swim trunks down. With Nick now impressively naked and the trunks in her hand she realized she had forgotten one crucial step: the condom.

Mouth dry, she clambered off the bed and rummaged in her beach bag until she found the box of condoms she had bought earlier in the day. Feeling a little panicked because she sensed the ambiance was deteriorating, she selected one at random. In the process a number of the packets flew onto the floor.

Nick slid off the bed. His light green gaze pinned her. "When did you buy these?"

The sudden grim tension made her freeze in place. "Yesterday."

"Then they're not for Corrado."

"No." She blinked at the idea that she would want to sleep with Robert. Although that concept was overridden by a far more riveting one. Nick was jealous of Robert. "I haven't slept with Robert."

Nick released her wrist, relief registering in his gaze. "Good."

The conversation was blunt and inconclusive, but the fragile hope that had been slowly, but gradually, growing over the past two days unfurled a little more.

With an easy, fluid motion, Nick picked up the box and began shoveling condoms back into it. "These look… interesting."

"I just grabbed the first box I found." And unfortunately, it seemed to be filled with an assortment of acidic colors and strange ribbed shapes.

As she attempted to tear open one of the packets, Nick picked her up with easy strength and deposited her back on the bed with him, pulling her close. The rough heat of his palms at her hips, gliding to the small of her back, urged her closer still.

The foil packet tore across. A black, ribbed shape emerged. Nick made a choked sound—a split second later he kissed her.

Swamped by a sudden sensual overload, she kissed him back. Long seconds later, she surfaced. The condom was still clutched in one hand; she had almost forgotten it. Not good.

Pulling free, she eased down Nick's body.

Obligingly, he allowed her to fit the condom. She had almost mastered the art of rolling it on when, jaw taut, Nick stayed her hand.

In a strained voice he muttered, "Maybe you should let me do that."

With an expert motion he completed the sheathing. Face oddly taut, he pulled her beneath him. Before she could protest, he kissed her, his gaze soft, his mouth quirked. "Sorry, babe. You can be on top next."

Babe. A quiver of pleasure went through her at the easy endearment. Entranced by Nick's heat and weight, his clean masculine scent laced with sea salt, it suddenly ceased to matter that her plan had been overridden, or that she'd had a plan at all.

She was with the man she loved with all her heart. As he came down between her legs in the intense, heated joining that seared her to her very core, she had a split second to log that, as inspiring as the book with its chapters of advice was, in that moment it ceased to have any relevance.

Lost in coiling shimmers of sensation with Nick, she had everything she needed and more.

A rapping at the door pulled Elena out of a deep, dreamless sleep. Nick was sprawled next to her, the sheet low around his hips, sunlight flowing across the strong, muscular lines of his back.

Suppressing the urge to ignore whoever was at the door and snuggle back against him, she glanced at the bedside clock, which confirmed that it was late, past nine.

Another rap had her sliding out of bed. Grabbing a white terry-cloth robe she found draped over a chair, she finger-combed her hair as she padded to the front door.

Her first thought—that it was someone from the hotel wanting to speak to Nick—died when, through a window she glimpsed two feminine figures. Both were casually, if elegantly dressed, which suggested they were guests.

It occurred to her that they could be clients from her seminar who'd decided that What Women Really Want meant some kind of license to pursue Nick.

If that was the case, she thought, becoming more

annoyed by the second, they were about to be disappointed. The days of Nick being pursued by gorgeous young things who thought he was free were over. Nick was no longer free: he was *hers*.

A rosy glow spread through her at the thought. Suddenly, wearing a bathrobe to the door had its upside. She was in Nick's cabin. It was obvious she had been in his bed.

She wrenched the door open and froze.

"Elena?" Francesca Messena, dressed in snug jeans, red heels and a filmy red shirt peered at her. "We knocked on your door—"

"When you didn't answer, we figured you must be here." Sophie Messena, cool and serene in an oversize white linen shirt and white leggings, frowned. "Are you all right? Honey, can you speak?"

Elena clutched at the lapels of her bathrobe, which had begun to gape, but it was too late, Sophie and Francesca had already zeroed in on the red mark at the base of her neck. "I'm fine. Never better."

Sophie glanced at her twin. "She doesn't look fine." Her voice turned imperious. "Where's Nick?"

Francesca gave Elena a sympathetic look. "We heard about the bet."

"What bet?" Elena attempted to block the doorway, but she was too slow. The Messena twins, both taller than her by several inches, and as lithe and graceful as cats, had already flowed past her into the hall.

"It wasn't a bet," a gravelly voice interjected. "It was a wager."

A split second later, Nick, strolled out of the bedroom dressed in jeans, hair ruffled, his torso bare. If there had ever been any doubt for the twins about what they had spent the night doing, it was gone.

Nick's gaze pinned her. Linking his fingers with hers, he drew her close, then casually draped an arm around her waist, holding her against his side. "Let me guess who told you. Eva."

Francesca picked up Nick's shirt, which was still lying on the floor from the previous evening, and pointedly tossed it over the back of a chair. "We're not at liberty to reveal our source."

"You should say sources," Sophie corrected her twin. "Then he gets left guessing."

Francesca lifted a brow. "Hmm. Obviously, you're much better at this than me."

Sophie folded her arms across her chest as if she was settling in for the duration. "I'm in retail. It leads to wisdom."

Nick's arm tightened around her. "Now that you've had your say and seen that Elena survived the night, you can leave. I love you, but you've got approximately..." He consulted his wristwatch. "Five minutes before we start making love again."

"Before what?" Francesca's brows jerked together. "You wouldn't dare."

Sophie ignored Nick and looked directly at Elena. "I heard the wager was for one night. You should leave if you want."

Elena was abruptly tired of the intervention, as well-meaning as it was. "It's not about one night," she said firmly. "We're in love. This is about the rest of our lives."

There was a ringing silence.

Francesca sent Nick a level look. "Then I guess congratulations are in order."

After breakfast, Nick suggested they leave for Auckland and his apartment, where they could be guaranteed privacy for a few days. The seminar was technically finished. There was no need for Elena to go to the main part of the resort, and since she wasn't a guest, she didn't have to check out. Her car was a rental, so it was easy enough to arrange to have it collected from the resort, which meant she could travel with him.

Elena was happy to pack and leave. Ever since the twins had burst in she had felt unsettled and on edge. Nick had been nice. More, he had been charming, but the good manners and consideration were oddly distancing.

She found herself desperately wanting him to revert to type, to be blunt and irritable or even outright annoying. She would rather fight with him than endure this sense of being held at arm's length.

On the bright side, they were going to spend the next few days together, before she had to fly back to Sydney, and Nick had mentioned a sailing holiday. It wasn't everything she wanted, but it was a positive start.

The drive to Auckland took three hours. Exhausted from an almost sleepless night, Elena dozed most of the way and woke as Nick pulled into an underground parking lot.

Minutes later, they walked into his penthouse, which had a breathtaking view of the Waitemata Harbour.

The penthouse itself was huge, large enough to fit three normal-size houses into, with expanses of blond wood flooring and an entire wall of glass.

Nick showed her to a room. Her heart beat a little faster until he dropped his bag beside hers. With relief she realized they were sharing his room.

Feeling happier and almost relaxed, Elena strolled through the apartment and checked out the kitchen before stepping out onto a patio complete with swimming pool and planters overflowing with tropical shrubs.

While she was admiring a particularly beautiful bromeliad with tiger stripes and a brilliant pink throat, Nick's arms came around her from behind.

"I have to apologize for my family. Sophie and Francesca should have stayed out of it."

She turned in his grasp and braced her hands on his arms, preserving a slight distance. "You mean stayed out of our relationship?"

"Uh-huh."

Elena frowned, but Nick had already drawn her close and the feel of his lips on the side of her neck was making it difficult to think. Just before he kissed her, it occurred to her that Nick had carefully avoided saying the word *relationship*.

Elena woke to the dim grayness of early evening in a tangle of sheets. Nick's arm was draped heavily across her waist, as if even in sleep he wanted to keep her close.

Easing herself from the bed so as not to wake him, she picked up his shirt, which was puddled on the floor, shrugged into it and padded to the bathroom.

The reflection that bounced back at her stopped her in her tracks. Dressed in the oversize shirt, with her hair ruffled, eyes still slumberous from sleep and faint red marks from Nick's stubble on her jaw and neck, she looked like a woman who had been well loved.

Her cheeks warmed at the memory of the few hours they'd spent in bed. The lovemaking had been sweet and gorgeous and very tender. While she hadn't gotten a chance to consult the book, mainly because Nick had snatched it out of her grip and tossed it over the balcony, she had gotten to be on top, *twice*.

Elena used the facilities, and washed her hands and face. Feeling absurdly happy, she studied Nick's razor and the various toiletries lined up on the vanity, and gave in to the urge to take the top off his bottle of aftershave. The familiar resinous scent made her stomach clench and her toes curl.

Strolling out to the kitchen, she poured herself a glass of water then walked through the sitting room, fingers trailing over sleek, minimalist furniture. The thought that this could be her home for the foreseeable future filled her with a rosy glow.

Although nothing was settled, she reminded herself. Nick was clearly still adjusting; they would be taking this one step at a time.

A familiar humming sound caught her attention. Nick's phone was vibrating on the masculine work desk in the alcove. Moving quickly, she snatched up the phone and thumbed the Off button. The absolute last thing she wanted now was for Nick to wake up and shift straight into work mode, ending their interlude.

Holding her breath for long seconds, Elena listened hard, but the only sound she could hear was Nick's slow, regular breathing, indicating that he was still deeply asleep.

She placed the phone carefully down beside a file, and froze when she saw her name on a sheet of paper that had slipped partway out of the folder.

Flipping the cover sheet open, she found a note from Constantine Atraeus, her boss, indicating that he was sending Nick materials he had requested.

The materials turned out to be her proposal for the seminar, the quiz she had devised *and a copy of the answer sheet.*

Knees weak, Elena sat down in the swivel chair pulled up at the desk and spread the sheets out.

The tension that had started at Francesca and Sophie's

intrusive questioning, followed by Nick's evasive behavior, coalesced into knowledge.

At some point, way before she had ever gotten to Dolphin Bay to run the seminar, Nick had filled out the quiz, marking every question with the correct answer.

The mystery behind Nick's high score was solved.

He had cheated.

Fingers shaking with a fine tremor, she double-checked the folder in case she had missed something.

Such as a real, fumbled effort at the quiz. Anything that might indicate that Nick Messena had an actual beating heart and not an agenda that was as cold in the bedroom as it was in the boardroom.

There was one final piece of correspondence. It was a memo to the manager of the Dolphin Bay Resort, granting him a week's leave covering the period of the seminar.

Clearing the way for seduction, because Nick had known how weak her defenses had been, that given long enough, she wouldn't be able to resist him.

Setting the letter down, Elena walked back to the kitchen, replaced her glass on the counter and looked blindly out onto the patio with its lengthening shadows.

Her head was pounding and her chest was tight. Why had Nick done such a thing? And why with *her,* out of all the women he could choose?

In her heart of hearts she wanted it to be because, secretly, he had always been falling for her, that he was just as much a victim of the intense, magical chemistry that had held her in thrall as she had been.

But the weight of evidence didn't add up to that conclusion. Three short flings with a man who was known for his tendency to go through women. A seminar Nick had maneuvered his way into, with her accommodation placed conveniently next door to his. The champagne and the carefully staged room, the scene set for seduction.

The fact that he had cheated on the quiz, as hurtful as that had been, was only the clincher.

A bubble of misery built in her chest. She had wondered what the invisible, unbreachable barrier was with Nick. Now she knew. It was his own well-established protection against intimacy.

The twins busting in now made perfect sense. They were his sisters; they knew exactly how he operated. They had been trying to protect her, trying to tell her that despite Nick's pursuit of her, he didn't intend to allow a relationship to grow. All he had wanted was the thrill of the chase, with the prize of a few passionate hours in bed.

She had stupidly ignored the twins and her own instincts, choosing to cling to a fantasy that she wanted, but which had no substance. In so doing, she had allowed Nick to succeed at the one thing she had vowed she wouldn't allow.

He had made her fall in love with him all over again.

Fifteen

Nick came out of sleep fast, drawn by the utter silence that seemed to hang over the apartment like a shroud and the taut sense that he had slept too long.

Instantly alert, he rolled out of the empty bed. The first thing he noticed as he pulled on his trousers was that Elena's suitcase, which he had set down beside the dresser, was gone.

Stomach tight, he finished dressing, grabbed a fresh jacket from the wardrobe and found the Jeep keys. As he strode through the apartment he automatically took stock. Every trace that Elena had ever been there was gone.

The knowledge that something had gone badly wrong was confirmed by a copy of the quiz, and the incriminating answer sheet, placed side by side on a coffee table.

Too late to wish he'd told Elena what he'd done, or that he'd shoved the file in a drawer out of sight until he'd had the chance to come clean. But yesterday, after the showdown with the twins and Elena's quiet statement that she was in love with him, he had been stunningly aware that it was decision time.

Either he committed to Elena or he lost her. But knowing that he should commit—more, that Elena needed him to commit—didn't make it any easier to step over an invisible line he had carefully avoided for years.

Grabbing his phone, he stepped out of the apartment and took the elevator to the lobby. He speed-dialed Elena's number. He didn't expect her to pick up, and he was right.

When the elevator doors opened, he strode out of the building and was just in time to see a taxi pull away from the curb and disappear into traffic. He controlled the impulse to follow her in the Jeep.

He already knew her destination. Elena was smart and highly organized, and as a former Atraeus PA she had a lot of contacts in the travel industry. She would have booked a flight out of Auckland. He could try and stop her, but he wouldn't succeed. She would be back in Sydney within hours.

Stomach coiling in panic he took the elevator back to his apartment and threw on clean clothes. Minutes later, he was in traffic. It was rush hour and took an agonizing hour to do the normal thirty-minute drive to the airport.

During that time he made a number of calls, but every time he came close to making a breakthrough and discovering what flight Elena had booked, he was stymied. Elena, it seemed, had invoked the Atraeus name and chartered a flight. Now, apparently, there was a code of silence.

He found himself considering the caliber of the woman who had started out as a PA, then turned herself into one of the Atraeus Group's leading executives. It was just one more facet of Elena's quiet determination to succeed.

Now she was leaving with the kind of quiet, unshakable efficiency that told him she wouldn't be back, and he couldn't blame her

He had made a mistake. It was the same mistake he had made twice before with Elena. He had been irresistibly attracted but had failed to be honest with her about where he was in the relationship stakes.

He had changed. The problem was that the process of change had been agonizingly slow and the urge to protect himself had become so ingrained that he'd closed down even when he'd wanted to open up.

The quiz had been a case in point. Instead of being up front with Elena, *exposing himself to vulnerability,* he had used his knowledge of the quiz to leverage the intimacy he wanted without exposing any emotions.

Now that very protective behavior had backfired, ensuring that he would lose the one woman he desperately needed in his life.

He picked up his phone and stabbed the redial. When Elena once again refused to pick up, he tossed the phone on the passenger-side seat and drove.

Nick stepped off the evening flight from Auckland to Sydney, carrying his briefcase.

He hadn't brought luggage with him because he didn't need to. He was in Sydney often enough that he owned a waterfront apartment just minutes from the city center.

Twenty minutes later, he paid the taxi fare and walked into his apartment. A quick call to the private detective he had hired earlier on in the day and he had the information he needed.

The tactic was ruthless but, as it turned out, necessary.

Elena had arrived on her flight and gone straight to her apartment. She had stayed in her apartment all afternoon, the curtains drawn. Twenty minutes ago, she had taken a taxi to an expensive restaurant where she was having dinner with Corrado.

Nick's stomach hollowed out at the report. Corrado's name was like a death knell.

He grabbed his car keys and strode to the front door. The mirrored glass on one wall threw his reflection back at him. His hair was ruffled, as if he'd run his fingers through it repeatedly, which he had. His jaw was covered with a dark five-o'clock shadow because he hadn't stopped to shave, and somehow he had made the mistake of pulling on a mauve T-shirt with his suit jacket. The T-shirt was great for the beach; it looked a little alternative for downtown Sydney after five.

Fifteen minutes later, he cruised past the restaurant, the black Ferrari almost veering into oncoming traffic as he saw Elena and Corrado occupying a table by the window overlooking the street.

Jaw clenching at the blaring horns, he searched for a parking space and couldn't find one. Eventually he found a spot in an adjoining street and walked back in the direction of the restaurant.

He was just in time to see a troop of violinists stationing themselves around Elena and Corrado and a waiter arriving with a silver bucket of champagne.

His heart slammed in his chest. Corrado was proposing.

Something inside him snapped. He was pretty sure it was his heart. In that moment he knew with utter clarity that he loved Elena. He had loved her for years. There was no other explanation for his inability to forget her and move on.

Too late to wish that he could have found the courage to tell Elena that.

His family had termed his behavior a dysfunction caused by the supposed betrayal of his father, but they were wrong.

The situation with his father had definitely skewed things for Nick. He had walked away from a lot of emotions he wanted no part of, but that still hadn't stopped him falling for Elena.

He had been hurt, but his dysfunction hadn't been his inability to fall in love, just his objection to *being* in love.

Dazed at the discovery that he had found the woman he wanted to spend the rest of his life with *six years ago* and had somehow missed that fact, Nick walked up to the table and curtly asked the violinists to leave.

The music sawed to a stop as Elena shot to her feet, knocking over the flute that had just been filled with champagne. "What are you doing here?"

"Following you. I hired a private detective."

Elena blinked, her eyes oddly bright, her cheeks pale. "Why would you do that?"

"Because there's something I need to tell you—"

"Messena. I thought I recognized you." Corrado pushed to his feet, an annoyed expression on his face.

Doggedly, Nick ignored him, keeping his gaze on Elena. "We didn't get to talk, either last night or this morning, and we needed to."

He didn't need to shoot a look at Corrado to know that he had heard and understood that they had clearly spent the night together. It wasn't fair or ethical, but he was fighting for his life here.

Reaching into his jacket pocket, Nick pulled out the original copy of the quiz he had attempted without the

answers and a letter he had written on the flight from
Sydney, and handed both to Elena.

The quiz contained the raw, unadulterated truth about
how bad he was at conducting a relationship. The letter
contained the words he had never given her.

He didn't know if they would be enough.

Elena took the crumpled copy of the quiz and the letter.

Breath hitched in her throat, she set the letter on the
table and examined the quiz first.

She knew the answers by heart. A quick scan of the
boxes Nick had marked gave him a score that was terminally low. It was the test she had expected from him,
reflecting his blunt practicality and pressurized work
schedule, the ruthless streak that had seen him forge a
billion-dollar construction business in the space of a few
years.

It was also, she realized, a chronicled list of the non–
politically correct traits that attracted her profoundly.
Alpha male traits that could be both exciting and annoying, and which Corrado, despite looking the part, didn't
have. "You cheated."

The hurt of finding the sheet seared through her again.
"I thought you used it to get me into bed."

A woman from a neighboring table made an outraged
sound. Elena ignored it, meeting Nick's gaze squarely.

"I did cheat," he said flatly. "I knew I wouldn't stand
a chance with you, otherwise. Things were not exactly
going smoothly and the opportunity was there to get you
into bed so we could have the time together we needed.
I took it."

Elena held her breath. "Why did you want time together, exactly?"

There was a small vibrating silence. "The same reason I arranged to be in Dolphin Bay during your seminar. I wanted what we should have had all along—a relationship."

Fingers shaking just a little, she set the quiz down and picked up the letter. Written on thick blue parchment, it looked old-fashioned but was definitely new and addressed to her.

Holding her breath, she carefully opened it and took the single sheet out. The writing was black and bold, the wording straightforward and very beautiful.

The flickering candles on the table shimmered, courtesy of the dampness in her eyes. Her throat closed up. It was a love letter.

Her fingers tightened on the page. Absurdly, she was shaking inside. She noticed that at some point Robert had left. It seemed oddly symptomatic of their short relationship that she hadn't noticed. "What took you so long?"

"Fear and stupidity," Nick said bluntly. "I've loved you for years."

He took her hand and went down on one knee. There was a burst of applause; the violins started again.

Nick reached into his pocket again and drew out a small box from a well-known and extremely expensive jeweler. Elena's heart pounded in her chest, and for a moment she couldn't breathe. After the black despair of the flight to Sydney, the situation was…unreal.

Nick extracted a ring, a gorgeous pale pink diamond solitaire that glittered and dazzled beneath the lights. "Elena Lyon, will you be my love and my wife?"

The words on the single page of romantic prose Nick had written, and which were now engraved on her heart, gave her the confidence she needed to hold out her left hand. "I will," she said shakily. "Just so long as you promise to never let me go."

"With all my heart." Nick slid the ring onto the third finger of her left hand; the fit was perfect. "From this day forward and forever."

He rose to his feet and pulled her into his arms, whispering, "Babe, I'm sorry I had to put you through this. If I could take it all back and start again, I would."

"It doesn't matter." And suddenly it didn't. She had been hurt—they had both been hurt—but the softness she loved was in his eyes, and suddenly loving Nick was no risk at all.

Epilogue

The wedding was a family affair, that is, both the Messena and the Lyon families, with a whole slew of Atraeus and Ambrosi relatives on the side.

The bride was stylish in white, with racy dashes of pink in her bouquet and ultramodern pink diamonds at her lobes.

Elena did her best not to cry and spoil her makeup as Nick slid the simple gold band, symbolizing love, faithfulness and eternity, onto her finger. When the priest declared they were man and wife, the words seemed to echo in the small, beautiful church, carrying a resonance she knew would continue on through their married life.

Elena's bridesmaid, Eva, on the arm of Kyle Messena, the best man, strolled behind them down the aisle. They halted at the door of the church and the press jostled to take photos.

Elena leaned into Nick, suddenly blissfully, absurdly

happy. "Let's hope they get the wedding story right this time."

Nick pulled her even closer, his hold protective as they made their way toward the waiting limousine. "No chance of a mistake this time. Pretty sure Eva's on record as saying she'll never marry, and Kyle's escorting her on sufferance. They're oil and water."

As brilliant and sunny as the day was, the wedding photos proved to be a trial. The Messena family did what all large families did; they argued. Sophie and Francesca were the worst. They loved Nick unreservedly, but they couldn't resist poking and prodding at him.

Their main issue was that they wanted to know what the aliens had done with their real brother, the bad-tempered, brooding, pain-in-the-ass one, and when would they be getting him back?

Nick had taken it all in good part, telling them that if they had an ax to grind over the fact that he had fallen in love, they would have to take it up with his wife.

Sophie and Francesca had grinned with delight, given Elena a thumbs-up and opened another bottle of champagne.

Halfway through the wedding dinner, which was held at sunset under the trees at the Dolphin Bay Resort, a guest they had all been waiting for arrived.

Tall, dark and with the clean, strong features that would always brand him a Messena, Katherine Lyon's long-lost son hadn't wanted to miss the wedding. Unfortunately, his flight from Medinos had been delayed, which meant he'd missed the actual ceremony.

Nick, who had gone to Medinos to meet with Michael Ambrosi just weeks before, made introductions.

Elena dispensed with the handshake and gave him a hug that was long overdue. After all, they were cousins.

After being thoroughly welcomed into the family fold, Michael took Elena and Nick aside and produced a small box.

Elena surveyed the antique diamond ring, nestled on top of the stack of love letters they had found in Katherine's attic, and finally understood why there had been so much fuss about it.

The pear-shaped diamond was set in soft, rich gold and radiated a pure, white light. The setting suggested that the ring was very, very old, the purity of the stone that it was extremely expensive.

Gorgeous as it was, Elena very quickly decided she much preferred the softness of the pink solitaire Nick had given her. "Aunt Katherine would have been proud to wear it."

Michael replaced the ring in its box. As Carlos's son, the ring was his to give to his future wife if he chose. It was just one of the many strands that now tied him irrevocably into a family that had been anxious to include him and make up for lost time.

As the sun sank into the sea, Nick pulled Elena onto the dance floor constructed beneath the trees. Illuminated by lights strung through the branches and just feet away from the waves lapping at the shore, it was the perfect way to end a perfect day.

A little farther out in the bay, Nick's yacht—the venue for their honeymoon—sat at anchor, lights beckoning.

Elena wound her arms around Nick's neck and went into his arms. "I have a confession. I used to watch you from the beach when I was a teenager."

Nick grinned. "I used to watch you from the yacht."

Elena smiled and leaned into Nick, melting against him as they danced.

No more unhappiness, no more uncertainty, she thought dreamily. *Just love.*

* * * * *

*If you liked Elena's story, don't miss a single novel
in THE PEARL HOUSE series from
Fiona Brand*

*A BREATHLESS BRIDE
A TANGLED AFFAIR
A PERFECT HUSBAND
THE FIANCÉE CHARADE*

*All available now,
from Harlequin Desire!*

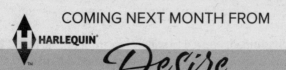